PROMICIDE

Zachary Graves

ISBN 979-8-9890408-0-3

First edition

Chapter 1

Nestled in a forested nook of Middle America lies Barbara Falls, a dot of a town named after the roaring waterfall that marks its eastern border.

Legend has it, in the 18th century, a love-struck explorer stumbled upon the isolated falls while on his way back to his hometown. To make clear the depth of his passion for his fiancée, Barbara Barbinson, he named the liquid landmark after her.

Today, Barbara Fallians often recite this tale to the few who happen to visit. Their beautiful town was built on love, they say, and just like the roaring of the falls, that love has never calmed.

What most of them don't know, however, is that the true story of Barbara Barbinson ends in the throes of another lover: death.

Poor Barbara's head was split down the middle by an axe wielded by the very man who wished her name to live on in eternity. As the police carried him off, the man raved of Barbara's incessant babbling.

The explorer was put to death, but his lover's prattle still continues to this day. Trouble is, no axe can cut through the babble of Barbara Falls.

After ten miles of thick tree cover, the lone road to and from the falls becomes Barbara Falls' Main Street, a charming thoroughfare of small businesses and foot traffic. Branching asphalt arteries lead to large, two-story homes, housing the town's 700-some residents in spacious, middle-class grandeur.

A drive down Main Street is a theme park ride through comfortable, stultifying, small-town America. Snow-white young mothers pushing their spawn around in a stroller. Sheriff Joe Matthews giving a group of teens a firm talking-to about their boyish mischief. Young ones walking to school and older ones sitting in the park, wondering where it all went so wrong.

The bucolic charm, however, is short-lived. The other side of Main Street once again becomes another stretch of all-encompassing forest, but this patch of woodland hides an institution most Barbara Falls residents wish wasn't part of their nice, little town.

Renowned psychologist Dr. Donald McVey

spent almost every Thursday afternoon traveling to this carnival of horrors, but the drive was still a fight against catatonia-inducing fear each time. Turning off the main road sent a shiver down the doctor's spine, and the sight of his final destination sent another shiver down the first one.

McVey shifted his car into park and stared up at the isolated cement building in front of him.

Shady Hills Mental Hospital.

He took a slow, deep breath, gulped down a swallow's worth of fear and gathered up the courage to exit his Audi 100.

It was a beautiful day outside Shady Hills. Shame that beauty couldn't make it inside its walls; the chilly aura of the hospital overpowered the sun's warmth. McVey shivered, buttoned up his beige trench coat, and walked towards the hospital's front door.

But it wasn't the long, dark car ride through the wilderness or the faded facade of the hospital that made McVey nervous. It was the man he was coming to see.

McVey had long ago given up all hope of curing the psychopathic maladies of the patient housed in Shady Hills' highest-security ward. Never in his long and celebrated career had he experienced anyone, or perhaps *anything*, like the man in Section D. He was the darkest soul he had ever encountered, darker than a recently paved blacktop slathered in matte black paint.

Still, the doctor thought it disrespectful to his beloved craft to give up on the job altogether. Thus, for ten years, he had made the weekly drive up to Shady Hills, fighting the urge to instead drive his car into the watery bliss of Barbara Falls.

There was one ray of light inside Shady Hills each week: the facility's receptionist, Nancy. For a moment, Nancy's toothy, winsome grin, proven capable of melting many a Barbara Falls man's heart, made McVey believe he was overreacting, that there was nothing to be scared of inside Shady Hills.

"Morning, Dr. McVey," Nancy said, lifting her head from the spiral notebook on her desk. She had been doodling, drawing spirals that led into other geometric shapes. "How are you?"

McVey felt unbridled lust twinge in his chest and nether regions, so he cut the conversation short, as he always did. "Very well, Nancy, but no time for small talk. Can you find a guard to escort me to Section D, please?"

Soon, a tall, afroed man in a fresh, white uniform was leading McVey down the elongated corridor to Section D. The ward had been created especially for McVey's patient, and he remained its only inhabitant. As they walked, the overhead lights became dimmer and dimmer. Hospital staff had once replaced the bulbs lighting the passageway, but stopped when they found each one hardly lasted a week before burning out. Whatever evil lay in Section D was so vast, it couldn't help but spill out.

"What an evil man," Dr. McVey thought out loud. "With a soul blacker than the blackest black cat. His very essence eats up the light around him."

The guard, who had a name but not one important enough to list here, rolled his eyes. He had listened to McVey talk about the man in Section D every week for the six months he'd worked at the hospital. "Black" this, "dark" that… truth is, it didn't help his nerves one bit.

"Section D is the only place fit for a soul such as his. I shudder to think what would happen if he ever came into contact with the sun," the doctor continued.

"Trust me, Doc, this guy ain't *ever* getting out," the nameless inferior said.

They passed through three increasingly thick, bolted doors of iron and steel, locking each door behind them as they entered. A guard in a wooden chair sat outside the fourth and final door. He stood up to greet the only visitors he received each week.

"Afternoon, Dr. McVey," the guard at the door

said.

McVey did not respond. He walked up to the steel door and looked through the small glass window into the padded cell inside. His patient lay huddled in the far corner of the room, wrapped in a blanket. A lump of pure evil, chained to the far wall by both legs. McVey swallowed his fear and nodded to the guard.

The doorman used his scanner card to open the last door, and McVey picked up the guard's wooden chair and walked in. The room, bathed in white, was sterile, imposing. The doctor stepped his way to the patient on the floor, the other guard following close behind. He plopped his chair six feet from the mass on the ground, the bane of his profession, the object of his sleepless nights.

"Hello, Benjamin."

The lump did not answer, nor did it move. Strange. McVey rarely saw the man in Section D sleeping. Most Thursdays, he was upright, waiting for the doctor, a contemptuous smile licking his lips.

"Benjamin, it's Dr. McVey. It's time for your weekly session."

Still nothing.

For the first time in years, McVey felt hope in the miserable pit of Section D. What if… his patient was dead?

The epitome of evil gone. Ten years of fear and dread over in an instant. A feeling flooded over him, a feeling forgotten, that of a six-year-old McVey, unwrapping a copy of the DSM-II on Christmas morning.

"Benjamin!" he yelled again, the gleeful tone mocking the mass on the floor.

"Something wrong, Dr. McVey?" the doorman asked behind him. McVey thought he heard the same joyous tone coming from the man's voice, as if he had left the patient's body there for McVey to find, to unwrap like his Christmas present so many years ago. What a beautiful fellow. He would have to ask him his name.

"Nothing at all," McVey said, smiling at the doorman. "It's time to wake up, Benjamin!"

McVey rose, knocking his chair over and swinging back his leg. He would open his gift the best way he knew how. His foot careening towards the psychopath's body, he remembered running towards the Christmas tree, mind alive with the wonders awaiting him.

But no satisfying crunch of bone accompanied the kick, only a light thud and a couple wool blankets flying towards the far wall. His gift was empty. Benjamin was gone.

McVey spun towards the door, realizing his mistake. An all-too-familiar contemptuous smile waited for him on the doorman's face.

"I think we're going to have to postpone this session, Doctor," the doorman said. His eyes were empty, devoid. Dead.

The man started to convulse, his body rocking with uncontrolled intensity. His mouth fell open before growing wider and wider. His blank eyes fixated downwards, on his enlarging gob. The mouth was giving birth, little brown hot dogs inching out from the inside.

But this was no cocktail party and those were no little smokies. They were fingers.

Two sets of them spilled from the poor guard's mouth, the virile digits grasping onto the man's chin and face. Fingernails dug deep and ripped claw-marks across brown skin. A quiet crack became the definitive crunch of snapping jawbone.

McVey looked to the other guard, hoping the man's extensive training in mental hospital security had left him prepared for a situation such as this. Instead, the guard stood huddled against the far padded wall, his eyes alive with fear, dampness spreading across his cream white pants.

With a beastly snap, the doorman's head split in two, spraying globs of red across the drab interior of the cell. The intruding hands were soon arms covered in blood and viscera. They pushed the body apart, shattering ribs with ease, cracking and snapping the man's interior until all that was left was a flabby pile of skin and skeletal fragments.

And Benjamin. He stood half-naked, hair shaggy, eyes crazed, a sharp piece of rib clasped in his hand.

"Just what the doctor ordered?" The man from Section D laughed, a maniacal surge of evil. The patient leapt towards McVey, thrusting the jagged rib through his neck and out the other side before he even had time to scream.

McVey felt the white heat of fatal indigestion in his throat. As he dropped to his knees, he stared past his ex-patient and into the eyes of a gleeful six-year-old boy, flipping through the DSM and gleaming with new knowledge of schizophrenia and sociopathy.

I should've asked for a football, the doctor thought before collapsing to the ground, pushing the rib even further into his trachea. A faucet of gore poured from the wound.

The guard in the corner, damp with piss, sweat and fear, watched as the bloodied patient smiled and crept towards him.

"Please, no! I have a kid!" the guard cried. "He's only three! He needs his poppa!"

"A kid, you say?" the killer asked.

The guard nodded in desperation, tears streaming down his face.

"Good. I love dessert," the patient said before

digging his teeth deep into the guard's jugular.

Nancy the receptionist, lost in her doodles, thought nothing of a man in Dr. McVey's beige trench coat entering her office until the moment she found herself being strangled by a large intestine. Her charming smile had no effect on the man from Section D; he strung her up from the ceiling fan and watched as drool and intestinal-noose blood dripped on her spiral drawings below, smearing the ink and ruining any chance of the piece one day being displayed in the Museum of Modern Art.

That year, a large chunk of Shady Hills' staffing budget had been rerouted by the federal government towards bombing the third world, so there was no one else alive to see the man from Section D get into Dr. McVey's Audi 100 and drive from the hospital, veiled by thick tree cover, towards the small town of Barbara Falls.

Chapter 2

In the spring of 1987, nobody in Barbara Falls could stop talking about how beautiful the weather was.

While this was partially due to their vapid lives lacking any and all profundity, it was also because this was a rare occurrence in the small town. Winters were tough in Barbara Falls. Middle America, famously surrounded by large bodies of water, is struck with numerous ice storms and endless flurries of white powder in the wintertime. The summer months, meanwhile, bring upon the town violent rain storms second-to-none in the world, except, possibly, in countries outside the United States.

But April? Perfection. The mid-60s temperatures would strip the town down to their bathing suits if not for the preternatural number of mosquitoes and leeches in the area. It was the only time of the year Barbara Falls teens even *thought* about hanging outside instead of at Hamburger

Heaven. They did not do so, however, as the outdoors rarely, if ever, provide you juicy, perfectly-cooked hamburgers.

The sunshine and blue skies provided the perfect backdrop for the end of the Barbara Falls High school year. Soon, the seniors would graduate and move on to their bright futures as attendees of state colleges, auto mechanics, and crack addicts. Yes, all 42 members of the senior class had a serious case of spring fever, and not the kind that caused skin lesions.

On the Thursday before prom, the beauty of April appeared to be at its peak. The light shined just right on drab, institutional Barbara Falls High School, obscuring its blemishes and bathing its faded tan paint job in a calming swath of golden yellow.

Nancy, the school's receptionist, however, kept her eyes fixed on the word search in front of her. Word searches were her go-to activity to pass the time. Crosswords and coloring pages just took too much brain power.

She had almost beaten today's aquatic-themed game, save for one word. Her eyes zipped around in search of any 'M' that might begin the word 'MERMAID.' M… M… M… where could it be?

"It's an *outrage*, I tell you!"

Nancy yelped in shock at the sudden squawking

in her ear. She knew who her unexpected visitor was before even looking up.

Mrs. Poughkeepsie. Her heart sank.

"Here I am, teaching Shakespeare. *Romeo and Juliet,* his best work. I'm reading out loud, and I notice Cheg here *doodling* instead of paying attention!" Mrs. Poughkeepsie said before Nancy had a chance to ask what happened.

Poughkeepsie's frizzy, unkempt hair sloshed back and forth as she talked, in time with the flapping pudge of her flailing arms. She reminded Nancy of a frightened turkey when she complained, which was always.

Behind her was Cheg Larson, the chief bad boy of Barbara Falls High. Today, like all days, he was dressed in a shit-eating scowl and denim from head-to-toe. The office was his second home; Cheg spent more time with the principal than with his own mother.

"I ask him, 'Cheg, do you have anything to share with the class?' 'Sure,' he says, stands up, and shows the class *this*."

Like Moses wielding the Ten Commandments, Poughkeepsie raised a spiral-bound notebook to Nancy's face. Scratched onto the lined page was a picture of Juliet staring out her second-story bedroom window. On the ground below, Romeo, tugging on his large, veiny member, sent a shower of semen towards the coy Capulet.

Cheg snickered behind her as Poughkeepsie's face glowed a watermelon red.

"Better watch her, Nancy," Cheg said. "I've got a dollar that says she'll take it home with her later."

Nancy, a sweet, young soul with a uniquely toothy, winsome grin proven capable of melting many a Barbara Falls man's heart, was not shy around the male anatomy, and the immaculately drawn Montague cock in front of her meant far less to her than finding her 'MERMAID.'

"I'm sorry, Mrs. Poughkeepsie. The principal is *really* busy right now, and I don't think he has time to punish Cheg. Besides, he's done worse," Nancy said.

"That's not *all,* Nancy! He stood up and started to act out his filthy drawing! He almost touched his wee-wee to poor Sandy van Thorpe's face! Such a sweet girl defiled by such an awful boy!" Poughkeepsie struggled through the story, finding it especially hard to spit out the word "wee-wee."

Nancy wanted to tell Mrs. Poughkeepsie that there were bigger fish to fry, specifically those with clam-shell bras and flowing auburn hair, but the bird hadn't finished her word.

"*Still* not all, Nancy! I stand up to take him down here, and he throws his desk across the room! It hit poor Douglas Whitehead straight in the face!

Look at his glasses! The boy probably needs an ambulance!"

Poughkeepsie presented shattered spectacles as evidence, a wave of arm fat providing an extra flourish. Nancy solemnly shut her book of puzzles, defeated, and walked towards the principal's office.

Behind her, Cheg pulled away from Poughkeepsie.

"Get your hands off of me! You're making my jean jacket smell like *bitch*," Cheg snarled.

Poughkeepsie gasped, her watermelon complexion deepening to cherry red.

Nancy walked into the office, shutting the door behind her to quiet the manic squawking outside. Framed doctorate degrees on the wall declared this as the workspace of Principal Forrest Wiener.

Wiener was a meticulous, organized leader. The endless snoozefests he called meetings were planned down to the second. He never lost a paper, especially his teacher observation forms, which he littered with nitpicky feedback.

Today, though, the man's desk was covered in hundreds of chicken-scratched sticky notes and papers. On the other side of the room, Wiener stared out the window, oblivious to Nancy's entrance.

This was Nancy's fifth year at B.F. High, and each year was the same. As the winter weather thawed, Wiener began to go soft, his self-importance traded for timidity. His meetings became impossible to follow, full of hems, haws, and moppings of his sweaty brow. In the fall, students were suspended for violations as minor as mispronouncing the man's name (properly: "whiner"), but come April, he locked himself in his office most of the day, refusing to punish students in all but the most egregious cases.

Each year, it was the talk of the teacher's lounge. Mr. Stannaker, the young, handsome history teacher new to the school this year, had joked to Nancy that Wiener suffered from seasonal erectile dysfunction. They both laughed, two poor souls lame-brained enough to find sophomoric penile humor funny.

Nancy stared at the curiously erect Wiener. She noticed a manila folder in his hand. She couldn't quite see what was scrawled across the front in red marker, but she could've sworn it read "KILLER."

"Principal Wiener?" she asked.

He kept his back to her. In the silence of the room, Nancy noticed he was whispering to himself, like he was murmuring sweet nothings to the glass panes in front of him.

"Uh, Forrest?" she asked again.

Wiener jumped. The folder dropped from his hand, and its contents spilled across the floor. He made no attempt to collect them.

He swept his head towards Nancy.

"Don't... call me that." Wiener's eyes were stretched open to the limits; one more centimeter and they risked popping from his skull.

Nancy realized her heart was beating faster than normal.

"Sorry... Principal Wiener. Cheg Larson is in the lobby. He assaulted a student again," she said.

Wiener turned back towards the window. "Can't you see that I'm in the middle of something, Nancy?"

"Yes, I can see that," she said. It didn't seem the right move to disagree. "But Mrs. Poughkeepsie is out there with him. Would you rather calm her down?"

For a few seconds, the ticking of a clock above the door was the room's only noise.

"Fine. Bring him in."

As soon as Nancy opened the principal's door, Poughkeepsie barged in and vomited out her story once again.

As she finished, her words hung in the room without a destination. Wiener still stared out the window. With no indication he had listened to her tirade, Poughkeepsie started to fume. She opened her mouth to start chastising Wiener, but Nancy slapped a hand on her shoulder to shut her up.

The silence felt eternal.

"I'd like to talk to Cheg alone," Wiener finally said.

The two women left, and Cheg crossed his arms, covering some of the thrash metal patches on the front of his jean jacket. He knew Wiener's tricks. He would start soft, asking why Cheg acted this way and what would make him behave. This would escalate to shouting and a quick suspension.

A suspension meant a day out of school. Fine with him. Maybe he'd drive to the town over and buy some cassettes.

"You're interrupting very important work," Wiener said, his back still to Cheg. It was a new line, one that caught the boy off guard.

"It looks to me like you're staring out a window." Cheg flashed his scowl.

"Oh, ho, *ho*, Cheg!" Wiener lurched his body away from the window and towards his visitor. "Do I look like I have time to deal with your juvenile shit?"

Large veins, ready to burst, littered Wiener's forehead. His eyes glared with unblinking intensity and his right foot performed manic paradiddles on the ground.

Cheg backed away, before realizing Wiener's game. He was trying to scare him... and Cheg Larson didn't *get* scared.

"The only shit here is the one I'm about to take

on your floor, Wiener," Cheg shot back. He glanced down and noticed papers sprawled across the office. Shadowed pictures. Floor plans of a large facility. Nervous scribblings.

Wiener gazed at Cheg with animalistic hatred. "Oh, another *zinger*. Such a bad, bad boy you are. Let me ask you something, Cheg. Have you ever seen evil?"

"What?"

"*Evil,* Cheg. Not the childish games you play, but pure… evil?" Wiener stepped towards Cheg, each pace pushing the boy deeper into the office's corner. "Because I have. I've stared into the black. Seen things so twisted, I wouldn't call them human."

Cheg found himself pinned against a wall. He began to sweat. This was a Wiener he'd never experienced before.

"And if you don't let me get on with my work," he continued. "You'll see it, too."

Wiener was close enough to Cheg's face to sneak a kiss. Cheg wanted to push the man away, call him gay, make fun of his hair, but he couldn't. He was frozen, the only warmth in his body Wiener's breath on his neck.

"Now, get out of my office." Wiener retreated, crouching down and arranging the scattered papers back into a neat pile. Cheg stood perplexed for a few seconds before heeding his advice.

Nancy was hard at work locating mermaids when Cheg tapped on her desk on his way out.

"There's something wrong with Principal Wiener," he said, before walking out of the office and the school, deciding he would take the rest of the day off.

Wiener saw him leave. He didn't care. He didn't have time to worry. He had waited for ten years, and the day was almost here. He turned back to his desk, staring at the now-organized folder.

Nancy wasn't mistaken. In bold lettering across the front of the manila file was one word.

"KILLER."

Chapter 3

The moment the clock struck three and the school bell echoed through Main Street, a rush of teens made the pilgrimage across the street to their after-school haven, Hamburger Heaven. They were eager to beat the rush and grab one of the mint-green vinyl booths for them and their friends.

"Cheers, guys," Chris Rothschild said from one of these booths, holding up a bottle of Hammer Cola that glistened in the afternoon sun. He had skipped his last class to ensure a piece of prime Heaven real estate. "One day closer to paradise."

Rothschild had said this each day since December. Still, everyone at the booth raised their Hammers high, clinking the glass bottles together and taking a long swig after. No sound sums up the end of another day at Barbara Falls High better than the satisfying "ahh" that comes after a long gulp of refreshing Hammer Cola.

And everyone in town knew Hamburger Heaven

was the place to hear it. At all hours of the day, under the watchful eye of James Dean posters and pastel color schemes, the burger joint was packed with babies, near-corpses, and everyone in-between, all ready to slip a dime into the jukebox and chow down on a delicious quarter-pound beef patty and an ice-cold Hammer.

The hamburger patties and fries sizzling in front of him made Rothschild smile. His afternoons here were the highlight of his day. Good food. Friends. Girl on his shoulder. What more could you ask for?

Rothschild wore his bleach-blond hair shaggy and unkempt. He paired it with a blue and yellow Letterman's jacket, helpfully labeled Rothschild. Prickles of facial hair poked from his chiseled chin, an all-American, pretty-boy mug tinged with grit. He was a boy you could take home to your mother, except that he might sleep with her.

Wrapped around Rothschild's shoulder was his girlfriend of two and a half months, Sarah Farrow. Sarah admired her nails, which were totally perfect. She was the only one without a hamburger in front of her; her bombshell dress for tomorrow's prom was already shrink-wrap tight and an extra millimeter of waistline could mean disaster.

Jimbo McKinney, however, worried not about his waistline. On the other side of the table, five quarter-pound patties lay in front of him, awaiting their masticatory demise. A linebacker on the notoriously terrible Barbara Falls High football team, Jimbo wore a faded gray graphic tee filled out by an equal amount of pudge and muscle. An Army crew-cut framed his gigantic head.

"Amen to that, man," Jimbo yelled from across the table, raising his hand for a high-five. The friends clasped their hands together in a brotherly fashion. They had been inseparable since the sixth grade. Jimbo was the one who got them in trouble, Rothschild the one who weaseled them out of it.

"So, Jimbo, who you bringing to prom tomorrow?" Rothschild asked, the first breach of the subject on all their minds.

"Fuck that, man. Going in with no date means Jimbo's gonna land some truly bitchin' pussy," Jimbo said.

"Ugh! You're disgusting, Jimbo!" Sarah said, looking up from her nails.

"Sarah, baby, you got me all wrong," Jimbo said. "You see, it's part of my community service! No girl deserves to be alone on prom night. All those lonely babes... they can come home with me!"

Jimbo laughed out loud, spraying beef granules all over Sarah and Rothschild. Sarah cursed back at him while wiping cow bits from her shirt.

Here they go again, Jenny Hibiscus thought, safely out of range two seats over from Jimbo. Between them was her boyfriend, Jeremy Vernon. She squeezed Jeremy's hand. He looked over at her and smiled.

That smile could swoon a dentist, and Jenny knew she was lucky Jeremy's calm blue eyes stared only at her. A bob of straw brown hair stopped just above his lovely eyes, and an oversized sweater matched his cuddly, lovable personality.

They were approaching their first anniversary as a couple, and Jenny had loved every moment. Well, at least every moment they spent alone.

A twinge of guilt crept through Jenny's chest. She had tried over the past year to find reasons to like Jeremy's friends, but it felt like fishing for pearls in a river of shit.

Sarah was nice enough. They shared a love for jewelry and Whitney Houston. But Jimbo and Rothschild?

When we leave Barbara Falls, I hope Jeremy leaves them behind, too, she thought. Jenny shared all her feelings with Jeremy, but this was the one secret she tried to keep locked away.

It wasn't working.

This wasn't Jenny's fault. She was genuine, kind even, towards Jeremy's friends. It was just very, very difficult to keep a secret from Jeremy Vernon.

In his youth, relatives and friends of the Vernon family were often regaled with remarkable tales about young Jeremy. The boy was so cognizant. So able to read people. Hiding Christmas presents was impossible; he would know when his mother brought them home, where she hid them, and what was inside the box. When he was seven, Jeremy asked his father if they *really* had to move away from Salt Lake City. Mr. Vernon hadn't even told his wife about the job offer out in Barbara Falls. It was like he knew *exactly* what they were thinking.

High emotional intelligence, his dad would say.

Not quite.

Jeremy could read people's minds.

In his head swam the hopes, dreams, and private thoughts of those around him. As a child, the never-ending rush of thoughts was a deluge, drowning his mind in stimuli, leaving him unable to focus. He once tried to beat the voices out of him, banging his head against the side-table in his bedroom until he lost consciousness.

That was when Uncle Mark found him. He helped him out. Calmed him down. Other adults murmured, gossiped about the crazy Vernon kid, but Uncle Mark kept him going. For a while, at least.

He never found a way to turn off his "gift." The voices inside others' heads burrowed into his unconsciousness at all hours, as certain as the setting of the sun or the continued popularity of

Loverboy.

But here he was, with college prospects and a date to the prom. Something approaching normalcy. He had achieved this by keeping the gift to himself, away from his friends, his parents. He even went against the advice embedded in the stream of voices. If Mom hid Christmas presents on top of the bed, he would instead look under it. They fell for it every time.

Jeremy wanted to tell Jenny. Truly. But he couldn't risk losing her. Dating a psychic is an intimidating prospect; you have no secrecy and they always know when you pass gas. It might be too much for her.

Jenny's feelings towards his friends, therefore, were no secret to Jeremy. He understood. Jimbo and Rothschild could be assholes. But they were also fun. Hilarious. Popular. And his oldest friends.

"Community service? As if, Jimbo! You couldn't even take home Crazy Jane over there!" Sarah said. With the hand not wiping cow goo from her sweater, she pointed towards the corner of Hamburger Heaven, where a rail-thin girl dressed in black sat all alone. Furious scribbles ran from the girl's pen into a notebook on her table, from which she kept her head only centimeters away. Black hair drooped onto the paper. The goth rock blasting from her headphones was audible from two tables away.

Everyone except Jenny broke into laughter.

"You kidding? I'd fuck the crazy right out of her," Jimbo snorted.

"Yeah, right! Crazy Jane is a total dweeb, and nobody can change that. And there's no *way* she'd let you sleep with her," Sarah answered.

"Wanna bet?"

"I'd bet my entire life savings that you can't do it. *Plus* free Hamburger Heaven for a month," Sarah snorted. "But if you can't have sex with Uber-Virgin Jane… you have to give me ten dollars."

The group fell silent. The stakes were on. Jimbo weighed his odds.

Sarah leaned towards him and twisted the dagger. "What are you, a pussy?"

Rothschild gasped. There was no way Jimbo could back out now.

"Fine. You're on, Farrow. I'll talk to y'all later… I'm gonna go plant the seed of sex now so I can *harvest* her later," Jimbo said. He took a quarter pounder in each hand and began to devour what remained of his five-course meal.

"Wait!" Jenny said.

Rothschild groaned. Jeremy was great, but his girlfriend was totally lame. Hot, but a super bummer. Whenever the group tried to have a bit of fun, she dragged her stupid moral compass all over it.

Women. Can't live with them, can't live without them, Rothschild thought, having a tendency to think in clichés.

"We shouldn't pick on Jane. She's in my math class. She's actually really nice," Jenny said. Her voice was a near-whisper.

"Why do you always have to ruin our fun?" Rothschild asked. "If getting a total loser's hopes up that they could go to prom with a football star, fucking her, and then never talking to her again makes Jimbo laugh, it seems to me he should do it. This is America, Jenny. America!"

Jenny fell silent and blushed into her lap. She didn't like stepping on others' toes, especially those of Jeremy's friends.

"Hey, watch it, Rothschild," Jeremy spoke up. He put his arm around Jenny's waist. "Maybe she's right."

Jimbo huffed, his mouth full of beef. He lived to make people laugh, especially at the expense of losers.

Stupid bitch. I'm going to fuck Crazy Jane whether you like it or not. And hopefully have a piece of you on the side, Jimbo thought. Jeremy perked up. His momentary loss of focus led a flood of thoughts into his distracted head.

Ugh, like, why can't she be cool like Jeremy? We're

just trying to have a little fun.

Maybe I could do my nails again tomorrow. No way I'm promming with grody nails.

In the caves, all cats are grey, in the caves...

Jeremy's always there for me. I'm so glad I'm with him.

His heart flushed. Hearing everybody's thoughts felt like a curse, but moments like these made it worth it.

I'm coming for you, Forrest.

This voice he didn't recognize. The thought was dim, distant, phantasmagoric.

He looked around the restaurant. His gift only worked on those nearby, and he couldn't see anyone he didn't know. And who was Forrest?

Jenny noticed him staring into space. "Is something wrong, Jeremy?"

Jeremy looked over at her. She was so beautiful. Her brunette hair tied back into a ponytail. Her bright-blue doe eyes shining with kindness. Imagine a weirdo like him with the most gorgeous girl in Barbara Falls. His worry melted away.

"No, babe. I'm fi..." Jeremy started, before a flash of white melted his entire vision.

In a blinding blast, the real world fell away. He could hear nothing, see nothing, feel nothing.

Except a voice. One that filled his whole consciousness.

Why are you in my head, boy?

Pure white shifted to the color of cream. He was in a room with walls made of cushions. Speckles and strokes of red interrupted the calming backdrop. Jeremy's soul floated above, there but not truly, lost in a dream forced upon him.

Then, he saw the bodies. Three of them. On the ground. Disemboweled, torn apart, floating in pools of their own gore. But he could not feel fear or disgust. The scene simply played in front of him.

Do you like what you see, boy?

Who are you?

You'll know soon enough.

And he was floating. He let go, dispersing his being towards the clouds above. The gruesome scene blurred, disintegrated, like film to flame. Supreme pleasure filled the spaces between, a joy heretofore unknown.

The air whirred. Shook. Distant white noise became louder, and louder, and louder and…

Snap!

Jeremy's eyes surged open as he whip-lashed back into consciousness, into Hamburger Heaven. Bright light dilated his eyes, first the left, then right. It was a flashlight, in the hands of a policeman. Sheriff Joe Matthews.

"He's awake," the sheriff said. Concern etched wrinkles into his youthful face.

Jenny muttered thanks to God behind the sheriff. Jeremy began to regain his sense of awareness. He lay on the ground, right below the booth he had occupied just moments before. Sheriff Matthews hovered over him, crowned by his friends and curious passers-by.

The sheriff switched off his flashlight and returned it to his duty belt. "What happened, Jeremy? We were worried."

"I… I'm not sure. I guess I… blacked out," he responded. His mind replayed the scene in the cream room. Seeing mutilated bodies while he was out? He would keep that to himself.

"I was just making my daily rounds," the sheriff said. He then motioned to Jenny. "When I saw this pretty lady lowering you to the ground, putting her jacket under your head. You're lucky you were with Miss Hibiscus here. She just jumped right into action, did exactly what you're supposed to do during a seizure."

Jenny blushed behind him. She never liked the limelight.

"Has this ever happened before, Jeremy?" Sheriff Matthews continued.

"No, never. Like I said, I'm not sure what happened."

Matthews patted him on the shoulder. He stood up and addressed the rest of Hamburger Heaven.

"It's all right, everyone! Go back to your burgers. Jeremy's fine."

Jeremy shuffled back into the vinyl booth. His head felt lighter, almost porous, but everything seemed to be back to normal. Jenny grabbed his hand.

"Shit, dude. Thought we lost you there for a second," Rothschild said, a forced smile failing to hide deeper worry.

"Let me take you home," Jenny said. "My car's at the school. I'll go get it."

Before Jeremy could protest, she got up and jogged to the entrance. The front door swung open violently as she approached, almost knocking her over.

Officer Robert Briggs burst through the opening, out of breath and frazzled. He was pudgy and in his late thirties. A thinning, close-cut hairstyle made his head look smaller than the rest of his heaping body.

"Oh, excuse me, Miss Hibiscus!" Officer Briggs said. He rocked a gentlemanly Southern drawl despite growing up in the Midwest. His eyes locked on Sheriff Joe Matthews.

"Sheriff, am I glad to see you!" he continued, caring not about the volume of his voice. "There's an emergency up at Shady Hills! Something real bad, Sheriff!"

Heads turned towards Briggs, eager for their second piece of panic in one day.

"Let's talk outside, Officer Briggs," Sheriff Matthews responded, feeling the anxiety grow around him.

"Bodies, Sheriff! Bodies on top of bodies! They're everywhere!" Briggs shouted.

A waitress gasped. A plate shattered in the back of the restaurant. Whispers broke the shocked silence. This was even more exciting than Christine Fairweather bringing a black boy to the homecoming dance in 1984!

"Quiet, Officer Briggs! Let's go outside!" Matthews stepped towards Briggs, who was now screaming.

"Mutilated bodies! Blood on the walls! Blood on the floor! Oh, God, it's horrible, Sheriff!"

Matthews had no choice. He slapped Briggs across the face. All was silent.

The sheriff turned to the restaurant and put his hands up in the air. "It's okay, everyone. The situation is under control. Everybody remain calm."

He latched onto Briggs' arm and dragged the man outside.

"Wow, Shady Hills! Isn't that the crazy-people hospital outside of town?" Sarah asked.

"Yeah, I hear they have a ton of padded cells in

there," Rothschild said.

"Yeah, cream-colored padded cells!" yelled Jimbo.

"Boy, that blood must've looked real red against those cream-colored cells," Rothschild replied.

Jeremy's guts sank to his legs. What if the mutilated bodies in his dream... weren't just a dream?

Chapter 4

In the basement of Barbara Falls High, Douglas Whitehead shook at the possibilities in front of him. A full ride to Yale? A Nobel Prize? Just the beginning. He smiled a crooked smile and adjusted his glasses, currently held together by electrical tape after a run-in with Cheg Larson's desk in fourth period.

Douglas was in the only place he could get any real work done. Sophomore year, he had slipped the janitor, a proud B.F. High alum, a fifth of Maker's Mark he stole from his mom. The exchange? Unrestricted usage of the school's basement.

Down here, he could focus on learning what he wanted to, not the arbitrary curriculum a committee of self-important imbeciles deemed worth teaching. The feeble-minded children unworthy of being referred to as his peers couldn't distract him with their name-calling and idiocy. His parents couldn't ask about his day or say they were worried about him. The only limitations were those of his own mind, and he decided he was close to transcending those as well.

Proof in point: the dog.

That summer, Douglas had found a German shepherd while walking home from school, its guts spilled across a quarter-mile strip, its eyes filled with a glassy look of acceptance.

Douglas scooped the leaking creature into a wheelbarrow and brought it home with him. He pieced together a makeshift respirator, enough to keep the dog from death's grip. And he began to create his masterpiece. Fido.

Fido would finally get him out of the black pit of Barbara Falls. Show off his unmatched genius. Paste on the lips of the world the name Douglas Whitehead. Fame, love, power: all in the dog lying on the operating table in front of him. If you could still call Fido a "dog," that is.

Fido's brain was now a supercomputer, capable of making intelligent decisions.

Its cast-iron teeth: more effective than the Jaws of Life.

Its troublesome lungs replaced by Douglas' homemade respirator.

Its tail a homing device. Its feet roller skates capable of reaching 65 miles an hour. Its fur glossy. Its temperament friendly. Fido was perfect.

Except, technically, Fido wasn't alive yet. Its heart was now a battery with a two-week life span, able to be controlled from anywhere with a remote switch, currently set to the off position and trembling in Douglas' hands.

Over the past three months, he had built technology the U.S. government would think inconceivable. Used untested mega-intelligent computer chips. Mined the Earth's crust for uranium-238.

And it all led up to this. The moment of truth. His finger hovered over the switch.

Had he thought of the potential consequences? Duh. Douglas Whitehead was incapable of overlooking anything. Sure, Fido's cast-iron teeth could cut through human flesh like a knife through marmalade. Yes, he'd installed laser devices into his eyes which served no scientific purpose. No, he wasn't *entirely* sure of the maximum range of his mecha-pup's radio-wave remote control.

These were minor concerns to Douglas. The worst-case scenario was an unstoppable killing spree for fourteen days, and who would really miss any of the scum residing in Barbara Falls? Jimbo McKinney, king of fart jokes and stuffing nerds into lockers? Losing him was a win for the world.

Besides, whether he won the Nobel Prize or slaughtered an entire town, the name Douglas Whitehead would be remembered forever.

His finger hovered for interminable seconds. It was time. He licked his lips and flipped Fido's switch, a loud click reinforcing his grand decision.

Douglas stared at his masterpiece.

Five seconds.

Then ten.

No, no, no, no, no, he repeated in his head.

He flipped the switch to off, then on, off, back on. The dog lay there, deader than the day he found it. His respirator still beat in its chest, performing warped CPR on a corpse.

Hopes, dreams, and a would-be legacy disappeared from Douglas like a Hammer Cola in the hands of a teenager. This should've been his big moment, his way out of this dead-end town. Now, it was nothing.

He screamed out and threw Fido's remote control against the far wall of the dank basement. It shattered against the floor as he did the same, tears drizzling from his face.

Head in hands and despair in mind, Douglas spent minutes on the cold concrete, until his defeat was overcome by an escalating discomfort.

He wasn't alone in the basement. He could feel it. Had someone stumbled upon his secret laboratory?

He looked up and met a pair of red eyes peering from the operating table. Fido stood, godly from Douglas' subservient position. Its metallic attachments shimmered under fluorescent light, its glossy skin capable of winning many a Best in Show ribbon.

"Fido… you're alive!" Douglas, incredulous, spurted out.

Fido nodded back.

The supercomputer brain worked. It could comprehend human speech.

Douglas righted himself and approached Fido. "Sit down, boy. I'm going to check you out."

Fido shook its little dog head.

"What do you mean, no? I'm your creator, Fido," Douglas said, eager for the respect so long denied to him.

Fido bared its teeth, stared at Douglas in defiance, and bolted from the operating table. It was gone before Douglas could comprehend what had happened.

"No, Fido! Wait!" Douglas started after his masterpiece, but knew it was hopeless. The nerdy scientist was no track star, and Fido's roller skates could outrun him without exertion even if he was. Oh God, what had he done?

No, no, no time to panic. His brain could solve any problem. He just had to guess where a razor-toothed, super-intelligent dog hybrid would head moments after rebirth. His brain churned. What did dogs love most?

Walks! Of course, dogs loved walks! Fido, even with a superhuman brain, would be out exploring, rolling around town, sniffing other dogs' butts and pissing on fire hydrants with enough power to tear the cast-iron straight out of the ground.

Douglas sprinted out of Barbara Falls High and onto his bike. With all the energy his stick of a body could muster, he rode towards home, to where he had found Fido in the first place. He just hoped the dog was headed there, back to its past life, to its previous owners.

He had to be right. He needed to be.

He wasn't.

Douglas Whitehead was a very intelligent young man, but all the great ideas swirling in his head consistently avoided one topic: the opposite sex.

It had thus not occurred to him that he should neuter Fido before he turned him into a robo-dog. Nor had it crossed his mind that when an animal wakes from a long slumber, it is really, really horny. Fido had used his super-sniffer to locate nearby mates, and it was ready to leave its super-seed inside anything it found suitable.

Unfortunately for Mr. Deakins, the school's biology teacher, that included Truffles, the pet guinea pig he kept in the back of the class. Fido unlatched Truffles' wire cage with its laser eyes and humped the poor thing to near-death until a super-spurt of potential mini-Fidos erupted from its core.

Mr. Deakins and his class were about to get an extra-credit lesson in biology.

Chapter 5

"Briggs, what the hell are you doing acting like that in front of all those teenagers?" Sheriff Joe Matthews fumed, a far cry from his usual charming disposition. He stood by Officer Briggs' patrol car outside the Hamburger Heaven.

"You didn't see the place, Joe! You didn't see all the blood!" Briggs answered. He leaned against the patrol car, shaking his head. "Nancy got a call from a janitor up at Shady Hills. Woman was out of her mind. Somethin' 'bout 'dead' this and 'strangled with a large intestine' that. Officer Davidson and I went to check it out. It was horrible, Joe. Just horrible."

Sheriff Matthews opened the passenger door of the car and reached for the radio.

"A psychotic man killing people at a mental hospital… I never thought I'd see the day. What's next, kids shooting up a high school?" Matthews asked. "Either way, you really dropped the ball back in there, Bobby. Our job is to keep people calm!"

He picked up the radio and called for Nancy, the station receptionist. She was a thoughtful, young woman with a toothy, winsome smile completely unlike the smile of anyone else in Barbara Falls.

"Yes, Sheriff?" she answered.

"Nancy… if anyone calls about what happened up at Shady Hills, tell 'em *nothing* happened. Hogwash, all of it," he said. "Over."

"Gee, I'm sorry, Sheriff. I guess things just got out of hand. Like I said, you didn't see it up there," Briggs said. He hated screwing up, which made doing it all the time even worse.

"Well, I think it's about time I go out there and do just that. And don't worry, Bobby. Shady Hills is out in the middle of nowhere. The man can't get far."

"I guess you're right, Sheriff. It wouldn't make no sense he'd get down here," Briggs said, as an Audi 100 carrying an escaped mental patient drove past them.

"Now, do you think you can brave Shady Hills one more time, partner?"

"I think so, Joe. There ain't much left in my stomach to throw up."

Matthews switched on the LED beacon topping the maroon 4Runner they called a squad car, and sped towards Shady Hills. As they pulled out, Jenny Hibiscus pulled into their parking spot and beeped her horn twice.

She tapped her fingers on the steering wheel of her Ford Escort. Her mind ran circles around itself. Her boyfriend just passed out and had a seizure in the middle of Hamburger Heaven! And what was worse... she couldn't stop thinking about prom! The one she loved was in danger, and, here she was, worrying about how it would affect her senior dance.

Jenny had never met anyone like Jeremy. He was so perceptive, caring, in touch with his emotions *and* hers. Most high school boys didn't even seem to realize the opposite sex had feelings, but Jeremy always seemed to know what would cheer Jenny up, even before she did.

They had first started talking in Mrs. Poughkeepsie's class last year. Jeremy would pass her notes with all the answers to the pop quiz... before Poughkeepsie had even announced it! He was a bright thinker, too, and Jenny loved hearing his opinions on the novels they would read in her class. She had coyly asked him if he wanted to start a study group together, and the rest was history.

Jenny Hibiscus couldn't imagine what her senior year at B.F. High would've been like without him. And she wanted their prom together to be as perfect as his charming smile.

Jeremy knocked on the passenger-side glass.

Jenny jumped out of her preoccupied stupor and unlocked the door. She calmed herself as Jeremy tossed his bag in the back seat and climbed in.

"How are you feeling?" Jenny asked.

"I'm fine. A little shook up, I guess," Jeremy said.

Jenny shifted the car out of park and began the five-minute drive to the Vernon house. "I just hope that never happens again."

"Don't worry," Jeremy said, as he reached for Jenny's right hand with a smile. She grasped it. "I'm good as new."

This was far from the truth. After waking from his tiny-coma, Jeremy felt something he had never felt before. Silence.

For the first time in his life, he stood alone in his own thoughts instead of those of others. Even now, his hand wrapped in Jenny's, the secrets of her mind remained hers to keep.

It was glorious. Every afternoon, after school, Jeremy slammed his bedroom door and spent any time he could away from the thought barrage of his parents. It was his only refuge. This was even better.

Jenny felt a difference, too, but chalked it up to a post-coma daze. She prayed he slept well tonight, so he could be her perfect prom date tomorrow.

"Do you remember anything from when you were out?" she asked.

"Nothing." Another lie. He couldn't stop thinking about the dead bodies in his mind.

"It's just... you were talking."

"What?" Jeremy rarely found himself taken by surprise.

"Something about a forest? You kept shouting, 'Who are you?' It scared me, Jeremy."

Jeremy's heart pumped. He had concealed his strangeness for years, and now, it was spilling from his orifices. He needed to leave this in the past.

"Hey. I feel fine," Jeremy repeated. "Take me through tomorrow's schedule one more time."

Jeremy grinned at Jenny. They had gone over prom night hundreds of times at this point, but he knew she loved talking about it.

"You better not have forgotten while you were out!" Jenny chuckled.

"It's all gone, Jenny! I don't remember a thing! Take it from the top!"

"Okay. Take notes if you have to." Jenny launched into their plans. 4:00 sharp at the Hibiscus house for photos. 5:00 dinner reservation for five at the most romantic spot in town.

"And the dance starts at 7. You'll be the best dancer in the whole school and knock me off my feet with your talent and charm," she finished.

"Obviously."

"Dance is over at 11," Jenny said, turning towards

Jeremy. "And then who *knows* where the night will go from there?"

Jeremy stroked Jenny's inner thigh with his free hand. "Well, we'll both be super tired. I'll drop you right home, so you can go to bed the second the dance ends."

Jenny laughed out loud. "Perfect!"

They pulled in front of Jeremy's house, a sizable, two-story home with bay windows and acres of weeded property out back. Jenny put the car into park, breaking her clammy handhold with Jeremy.

"I love you, Jenny." Jeremy had told many lies today, but this was not one of them.

Jenny blushed. She often did when talk of love came up. Jeremy loved this humility; Jenny was beautiful, but she didn't use it to her advantage or think more of herself because of it. Instead, she was genuine, caring, and kind. High school is a time of narcissism and insecurity, but Jenny didn't seem to have a speck of either in her perfectly proportioned chest.

"I love you, too," she said. She leaned in for a kiss. Their lips met. The warmth of love and barely-controlled teenage lust humidified her Ford.

Jeremy got out of the car, blowing her another kiss as he grabbed his bag out of the back seat. "See you tomorrow, my prom queen."

Jenny blew a kiss back and drove off towards her

own house.

Once inside, Jeremy tip-toed his shoes off and crept the front door shut. His dad was arguing with someone on the phone in the kitchen. He hoped Sheriff Matthews wouldn't tell his parents about the Hamburger Heaven episode. He didn't want anyone else worrying about him.

He sneaked up the stairs to his bedroom and shut the door. Beautiful peace and quiet awaited him.

His parents weren't bad people, or even bad parents. After an entire day of putting up a front of normalcy for his peers, though, Jeremy needed time away from other people's minds and concerns. His father's, especially, as they were too often about him.

His dad was a doctor, and even while he explained Jeremy's abilities away with medical jargon, it was clear they disquieted him. More superstitious parents would have taken Jeremy in to be tested for ESP, maybe even used him for a slice of fame. Not Dr. Vernon. To him, everything had a logical, scientific explanation, and any wife or kid who thought differently could keep quiet.

Jeremy missed Uncle Mark. In his bedroom back in Salt Lake City, Uncle Mark would tell him stories of other people with special talents. They would practice Jeremy's abilities, play guessing games and attempt to "contact" people from beyond his normal psychic reach.

Uncle Mark made him feel less like a freak. He was instead a superhero, someone with a gift that could help the world.

His dad wanted none of it. Jeremy's constant talk of psychic powers made Dr. Vernon cut all ties with his brother. Uncle Mark was no longer welcome at their house, and, soon after, the family moved to Barbara Falls to get even further away.

And now, Jeremy was a normal teenager, with prospects of college and a successful life. In Dr. Vernon's eyes, it was a job well done. Jeremy's childish fantasies had died away, like all such stories should, to make room for dreams of financial stability and ownership of real estate.

Jeremy thought of Uncle Mark, wondered what he might say about today's incident. He could have helped Jeremy, or at least helped him feel less alone. Instead, his father had whisked him away to this isolated town, cut him off from his only glimmer of hope. Veins of resentment burned in his chest.

He walked towards his bed, slipped off his backpack, and let it fall to the ground. He let the anger pass; this room was his safe space, the only place he could exist as his true self.

Today, however, his safe haven would be sharply, deeply penetrated.

Dizziness struck with sudden intensity. Jeremy

reached for the footboard of his bed, but his arms went numb, prickling and separating themselves from the rest of his body. The corners of his eyesight tunneled inwards. His field of vision narrowed instant by instant. He was falling. Falling.

He felt a sharp, cracking sensation, and then he was out.

He was no longer in his room. He was walking, down a dusty trail of dirt. Mobile homes flanked the path, trailers dumpy and well-worn. Potholes half a car deep littered the road. Black oaks blotted out the light from the sun.

Jeremy recognized the area. This was the strip of mobile homes on the outskirts of town. The side of Barbara Falls he and the others more fortunate avoided, made fun of. Poor man's land.

Yet here he was, walking. Slowly with a heavy step. No, it wasn't *him* walking. He was under the control of someone else, a marionette unable to move his own muscles. Forced forward by a power outside himself.

And what was wrong with his hands? His unblemished, boyish palms were now rough, choppy, cracked. Bloody knuckles gave birth to plump, aged fingers.

Then it struck him. This was another vision. And instead of getting the aftermath of the chaos, he had a first-person seat to the main event. His heart jumped at the thought, until he remembered he had no heart to do any jumping.

Who are you? He thought as loud as he could.

The heavy stride halted, then continued unperturbed. *Oh, back again, eh?*

You brought me here.

Young man, I have more important things to do than mess around with some infant.

Tell me who you are.

I could ask you the same question. Now hush. You're tuned in to 66.6 Death-FM. Sit back and enjoy the show.

They approached someone. A boy, standing on the side of the dirt road, something like a remote in his hands, looking around frantically. As they got closer, he realized who it was.

Douglas? Douglas Whitehead was a favorite target of Jimbo and Rothschild's mayhem, a scrawny nerd whose head knew well the interior of many Barbara Falls High toilets. Jeremy's ethereal stomach churned.

Oh, you two are acquainted? How sweet.

Douglas looked over at the man coming towards him. His pimply face wore confusion as he stared at the approaching stranger.

"Excuse me, sir. I appear to be lost. I was wondering if you could help," the man said. The voice boomed through Jeremy's mind. It was foppish, well-to-do, nary the slightest trace of menace.

"Uh, okay. What are you trying to find?" Douglas asked. They were now only feet from each other.

"I'm looking for the small intestine."

Douglas' look of confusion intensified tenfold. "Huh? What did you..."

He didn't have time to finish his sentence. The man plunged his hand deep into Douglas' unsuspecting stomach, like a bowl of excessively bloody chocolate pudding.

A surge ran through Jeremy's soul, a primal, electric excitement. He realized he was feeling what the killer felt, tapped into his unmoored psychopathy.

No, no, no. Don't let yourself get lost in him.

With ease, the man rifled through Douglas' innards, searching through organs, trying to find a favorite candy in a Halloween sack. He maneuvered with mastery. This wasn't the first time he had fingered the inside of another man's digestive system.

Jeremy felt sick. Douglas felt immeasurably worse.

The man pulled a juicy strand of intestine out of Douglas' new orifice and raised it to his mouth. He bit down hard. A squelching sound came with the chomp, and a dribble of mushy, half-digested food slopped onto the gravel roadway. Douglas dropped to his knees, unleashing more intestine along the way.

An acrid, metallic taste lit up Jeremy's spirit mouth. *Oh, God, I can taste Douglas! Get me out of here!*

Sorry, all patrons must remain seated until the smashing finale.

Douglas fell from his kneel and collapsed to his side on the rough ground. Jeremy's vision shifted downward. He saw a pale, fading look of fear on Douglas Whitehead's acne-scarred face.

And a steel-toed combat boot lifting towards the sky.

The boot thrust towards the ground, honing in on Douglas' face like a spider. The impact of steel on skin shattered the boy's skull to dust. Teeth shot from his gums and scattered across the street like loose change. The man brought his foot down again and again, until brain matter leaked from the boy's eyelids and his blonde hair was dyed permanently blood red.

Let me out, let me out, let me out. Jeremy repeated his mantra. It was all he could do.

Shut up in there. You're ruining my fun. The man crouched to the ground and picked Douglas' brain in the most literal sense. Grasping tight, he snapped off a foot of spine and lifted it to his mouth, slurping spinal fluid with glee.

Let me out! Let me out! Let me out!

SHUT UP!

The man's thoughts carried with them a force. Jeremy felt himself lifted from the foreign body in a sudden rush of headwind.

Snap! Jeremy was back in his room. His head throbbed, like the man was still inside him, struggling to get out. His vision fading back in, he realized he was resting his head in a pond of blood.

Oh my god. I'm covered in Douglas.

Standing up, he saw his bedpost speckled in red and realized what really happened. The crack he felt as he lost consciousness wasn't just in his mind. He put his hand to his temple and found a sticky wound. A shock of pain whipped through his body at the slight touch.

But he was alone. Safe. No Douglas… and no killer.

He spied the phone sitting on his headboard and ran to it. He rushed, dialing a 9, a 1.

Wait. What would I tell the police? That I saw Douglas Whitehead die in a vision? They'd lock me up for sure, he thought. *I'm supposed to be acting normal... and it's not like they could do much for Douglas anyways.*

He set the phone back down on its headset. Thoughts whirled through him as he tapped his fingers on his headboard. He'd learned nothing useful about the killer. The man had rough hands and sounded educated. Not exactly enough for a police sketch. And Douglas seemed like a random target.

He forced himself to calm down. If he had no information about the killer, that meant the killer had no information about *him*. He was safe. And with prom on the horizon, this was no time to get chummy with a serial killer.

Besides, maybe it was all in his head. It was possible, right?

But a pounding feeling in his gut told him this was just the beginning.

Adding insult to horrific, brutal injury, Douglas Whitehead had correctly guessed where Fido was heading. He just showed up early.

Douglas' killer happily munched on the boy's colon, his favorite human delicacy, until a firm growl came from behind him. He turned around and gazed upon his victim's final masterwork.

Fido was even more glorious in the setting sun. Its razor teeth, caught in a snarl, glistened as brightly as its shiny, healthy fur. The laser technology housed in its eye holes honed in on the bloodied killer, ready to blast through skin and bone like scratch paper.

Most would soil themselves in fear at the sight of such an amazing, hellish creature. The man from section D, however, saw one of the parts of life he missed most while locked away: puppies.

"Oh my God, boy, you're *adorable*! Come here, puppy! Let me scratch those scary ears of yours!" The man's high-class demeanor dissolved into the inanity of a mother talking to her stupid, worthless seed.

Fido's laser-sights switched off. Skating towards the killer with apprehension, its ears flopped down from their alert positions. The killer gushed praise at the dog, clapped his hands and ushered it over playfully.

When they met, the man covered the dog with a flurry of pets. He scratched its ears. Rubbed its belly. Ruffled its fur. Soon, Fido tackled the killer onto the ground, licking his face with love. Douglas' butchered corpse lay forgotten nearby, as unloved in death as it was in life.

A heartless, iron-fisted killer. A robotic dog with teeth of steel and roller-skate wheels. A match made in Hell.

Chapter 6

The next day, Barbara Falls was buzzing. Not because of the death of Douglas Whitehead, as no one, including his parents, had noticed, but because today was the day of the Barbara Falls High Senior Prom.

Throughout the city, each member of the senior class was preparing for the biggest night of their young lives.

Cheg Larson spent his afternoon in the Barbara Falls Cemetery, as he often did on days he skipped school. In the graveyard, there were no dickhead adults telling him what he couldn't do: he could hang out, drink, smoke, and blast cassette tapes to an audience of corpses as loudly as his black heart desired.

His wasted days with the dead were often spent with his best friend, Pat van Martens. Pat, a 1984 B.F. High graduate, worked at the local car repair shop during the day and binge drank at night. Growing up, Pat lived next door to Cheg. It was

Pat who showed him Venom's *Black Metal*, and Cheg had worn a patched jean jacket ever since. On days off from the repair shop, the two would blast S.O.D. and Overkill in the graveyard and shit-talk the dumb fucks who lived in their town.

Today, though, Cheg's only company was dirt weed and his stereo, blasting *Ride the Lightning* at top volume. There was a little piece of Cheg's heart that was upset he didn't have a date to the dance tonight, though he'd never admit that to anyone. He dreamed of a badass chick, platinum blonde hair, leather head-to-toe, roaring up on a bike and fucking his brains out before riding him to the dance, where he could show up all the little pricks with their ugly, boring girlfriends.

Still, he was looking forward to the dance tonight. He'd stolen a fifth of Jameson from his dad's stash, and he planned on wreaking some havoc on his personal hell before he graduated and never looked back. He took a puff on his joint, smiled, and let "Trapped Under Ice" wash over his denim-clad body.

One of Cheg's most hated classmates, Matt Brady, celebrated in a more traditional fashion. Mr. All-American was hanging with his buddies, Sam Berry and Brad Fahey, star running back and wide receiver of the Falls' football team. Matt was the quarterback, and despite the team's win-free record, the three of them had enough confidence to kill a motivational speaker.

Matt and Sam were in the running for Prom King, and both of them were determined to make Matt win that title. They put the final touches on their attire, matching white tuxedos and black bowties, as they had been doing for the last two and a half hours. You can't rush perfection, especially when you're accompanying three of the hottest babes in Barbara Falls to the dance.

The suit of Korean exchange student Dick Wong-Dick, however, was far from perfect. The tailor had seemingly misinterpreted the word "black" for "blech," dressing Wong-Dick in a vomit-orange disaster only acceptable for clown school and blinding nearby birds.

Wong-Dick had arrived in Barbara Falls that fall and, by now, was used to this sort of treatment. Despite speaking perfect, barely-accented English, everyone in the town looked at him in utter confusion whenever he spoke. He would order a hamburger and receive directions to the local Chinese restaurant. He would ask a question in math class and receive an A-plus.

Yes, America had been cruel to young Wong-Dick, from the moment he learned from the airport immigration agent that every syllable of his name was a synonym for "penis." The students of B.F.

High called him Bruce Lee, made karate poses at him in the hall, and talked about his "tiny wong-dick" in class as if he didn't understand them. It infuriated him, and he was very ready to be back in his hometown of Seoul.

Even so, Wong-Dick couldn't help but feel hopeful about tonight. Koreans did not celebrate prom, but based on the movies he'd seen, it was clear the night was a magical evening where even the least popular could get laid. Thus, he bought a suit, cologne, mousse. With only one month left in this godforsaken town, Wong-Dick was ready to lay it all on the line tonight.

Jimbo McKinney spent most of his day getting ready. His bright blue tuxedo looked perfect and his buzz-cut was even on both sides. He did 200 push-ups before dressing to make sure he looked extra ripped. After getting dressed, he spent fifty-two minutes staring at himself in the mirror. He looked *good.*

Whether it was Crazy Jane or another lucky nubile babe, Jimbo knew he would be getting some action tonight.

The only action Douglas Whitehead was getting was from a pack of crows, who made a midmorning feast of his decaying body. It was the most anyone had ever touched Douglas' body, and he would've appreciated it if his brain wasn't splattered across

County Road 13 like a failed omelet.

The only other teenager in town without sex on their mind was Sandy van Thorpe, valedictorian of the senior class and head of the school's prom committee. Sandy rushed around the school gymnasium, preparing the place for tonight. This year's theme was "A Night Under the Stars," and to achieve that magical effect, Sandy and her two prom committee slaves were hanging hundreds of glittery, wooden stars from the gym ceiling.

Her two servants, tomboy Rachel Severinsen and her boyfriend Corey Jones, received this punishment after setting off a stink bomb in the women's restroom. It was Rachel's idea, but Corey loved it. The couple got off on causing a little trouble. Nothing too serious, but enough to keep life interesting. Unfortunately, they had thrown the stink bomb into the ladies' room as stuck-up bird Mrs. Poughkeepsie was inside, washing her hands.

For two long weeks, Sandy van Thorpe had ruled over Rachel and Corey with an iron fist. They had cut three hundred stars out of wooden planks, set up every chair and table in the gymnasium, listened to Sandy debate herself on the ratio of dancing space to seating space, mopped and swept more times than the Barbara Falls janitorial staff had since the place was built, and even got the bitch coffee.

But tonight was the night the Van Thorpe Reich would be toppled to the ground, and Rachel and Corey had a little prank planned to celebrate.

Sandy had put her heart and soul into her Prom Committee work. No, she didn't have a date, but it would still be the best darn dance in Barbara Falls history. It was also the *coup de grâce* for Sandy's college application: 4.1 GPA; president of the Student Council, chess club, yearbook, newspaper, cross-country team, National Junior Honor Society, and the underwater botany club; and now, prom-planning extraordinaire. She expected an acceptance letter from Stanford any day now.

She was a girl with big dreams, and she wasn't afraid of pushing anyone else out of the way to get to them.

That included Leslie Deakins, who was currently at the hair salon. Leslie was the Vice President of Student Council, and when Sandy told her she didn't need to be part of the prom committee, nothing could have made her more happy. She could now avoid the abominable Sandy for a few days *and* be at the dance without having to clean tables or make sure no one put rum in the fruit punch.

She could keep her focus on what mattered: Alex Spence.

High school had not been easy for Leslie Deakins.

Sports weren't her forte; her extracurriculars were Student Council and drama. Blistering acne plagued her face. Her glasses were thick enough for a World War One vet. Her messy, curly hair could only be tamed into a sloppy bun with professional help, and her rail-thin body precluded any and all curves. The cherry on top? Her father was the biology teacher. No witty sense of humor or cute, dorky laugh could fix her diagnosis: a fatal case of the single life.

Enter Alex Spence. Junior-year transfer from Indiana. Big blue eyes the size of the moon and kindness just as wide. In the fall, the B.F. High drama department put on *Arsenic and Old Lace.* Leslie played murderous aunt Abby Brewster, and Alex got the role of her brother Teddy. Backstage, they shared laugh after laugh. Leslie fell head-over-heels harder than a deer on a date with a windshield.

To ask her out, Alex had somehow learned her locker combo and set up a flower-laden display inside, along with a note: "Sorry for breaking and entering. Make it up to you at Hamburger Heaven?" Her heart fluttered like a butterfly in the midst of a flutter.

On their first date in early March, Alex wore a goofy sweater, bright green and scratchy. They chuckled about it in the booth and held hands as they walked home together. Leslie had wanted to spend every moment with him ever since.

And tonight was the night. She wanted to make the evening super special, and she was ready to give him something she'd never given anyone else. If everything went as planned, they'd exchange their V-cards before the night was over.

Sitting at the salon alongside two other drama girls, the mere thought gave her special, sexy goosebumps. She was nervous, but there was no one in Barbara Falls, or maybe even the world, she'd rather do it with. The dance couldn't come fast enough.

One prom-goer who would not be giving up her virginity tonight was Sarah Farrow, as she misplaced it two years ago and had made no attempt to get it back since. Rothschild wasn't the first, but he was her lucky man tonight. Sarah had bought a dress that was spectacularly easy to take off, even for him.

Hope you're ready, Chris. She stared at herself in the mirror, perfecting her makeup. She was at the Hibiscus house, getting ready with the best friend she'd ever had in the last three months. Her pink dress was glorious and bejeweled, fit only for an Indian princess or the prom queen. She planned on becoming one of them tonight.

She had unleashed an entire bottle of extra-strength hair spray into Jenny's bedroom; lighting a single candle would blow up the entire block. Her coif was now as perfect as the rest of her.

"How do I look, Jenny?" Sarah walked into the bathroom, where Jenny sat on a footstool, finishing up her hair. She took a quarter-turn in her jewel-laden dress and brought forth an epileptic barrage of sparkle.

"Oh my *God,* Sarah, you look beautiful! Rothschild's going to love it!" Jenny beamed.

"Thanks. I *totally* made the right decision. I'm *so* glad I bought five dresses instead of four." Sarah walked over and put her hands on Jenny's shoulders, staring into her eyes through the mirror in front of them. "Jeremy's going to flip when he sees you, too."

"I hope so," Jenny said, curling her hair. "Yesterday in Hamburger Heaven scared me, Sarah. It really did."

"Well, duh, Jenny. It scared all of us. It was, like, pretty scary." Sarah wrapped her arms around Jenny's neck and kissed her on the cheek. "But stop worrying. Everything's going to be perfect. Jeremy probably just ate school lunch, and his body, like, couldn't handle it."

Jenny laughed. "You're right. I just can't stop thinking about it."

"Well, snap out of it, girlie! Dinner is in two

hours! It's time to get stoked!" She ran to the bedroom and punched the play button on Jenny's cassette deck. The ageless drum break of Whitney Houston's "I Wanna Dance with Somebody" exploded into the room.

"Come *on*, Jenny! This is my favorite song!" She ran to the bathroom and dragged her off the footstool.

"And when the night falls, loneliness calls!" Whitney crooned as Jenny and Sarah jumped around, sang into hairbrushes, and shook their groove things.

It was a moment of complete, ecstatic happiness, where time melts away and this mysterious universe of ours feels like home.

They would learn later not to take these for granted.

Jeremy used his mother's foundation to cover up the gnarly scar on his forehead. The color wasn't perfect, but he could play it off.

Oh, is there a bump on my head? Weird! Hang on, Douglas Whitehead got torn to pieces last night? Well, imagine that!

He'd gone all day without another visit from the psychotic mind-killer. A night's rest even sparked his mind-reading skills back into action; his mother's worries over the scar on his head and worst-case prom scenarios were more filling than his breakfast.

On the drive over to Jenny's, he spent more time looking at his forehead in the rear-view mirror than at the roads. He pulled up to Jenny's house as Rothschild was driving away in his beat-up pickup truck. Sarah waved from the passenger seat, and Rothschild flipped him the bird with a laugh.

Jenny's father opened the front door before he even knocked. "Well, there he is, the man of the hour. How ya doin', Jeremy?" Mr. Hibiscus had always liked Jeremy; he thought it each time he came over.

"Pretty darn excited, Mr. Hibiscus. Is Jenny ready?" Jeremy asked.

"Close, I think, but looks like you'll still have a few minutes with us old-timers," Mr. Hibiscus said. The man had a fuzzy mustache and formidable collection of sweater vests.

"Sounds like time well spent to me," Jeremy said. They shared a laugh, the tense half-chuckle only shared between a father and the young man who's having sex with his little girl.

Jenny's mom came in from the kitchen with a tray of cookies in her oven-mitted hands. "Oh, hello, Jeremy! I didn't hear you come in!"

"Hi, Mrs. Hibiscus. Boy, those cookies sure do smell delicious," Jeremy said.

Mrs. Hibiscus frowned. "Well, I don't see why

they would, Jeremy. They're made of plastic."

Above them, Jenny stepped down the stairs in her flowing navy blue dress. Jeremy and the Hibiscuses swept their heads in her direction as she entered and spouted a barrage of praise, as if she wore a halo on her head and was accompanied by a troupe of trumpet-playing cherubs.

"Oh my god, *Jenny!*"

"Wow..."

"My princess..."

Jenny blushed, as she was wont to do. "Oh, stop."

Jeremy walked over, took her hands in his, and stared into her bright eyes, the only blue in the room more striking than that of her dress.

"You look amazing," he said.

"You don't look so bad yourself," she said. In her mind, she asked herself what had happened to his head.

"Oh, you two are positively adorable," Mrs. Hibiscus cut in. "Let me find the camera." She threw the tray of cookies on the couch and ran off towards the kitchen.

Corsages and boutonnieres were exchanged. Mrs. Hibiscus took shots a professional photographer wouldn't have thought of. Mr. Hibiscus watched Jeremy run his hands all over his little sweetheart. They both told the young couple to be safe hundreds of times before they escaped to the haven of Jeremy's two-door coupe with just the right amount of time to get to their romantic dinner location.

Hamburger Heaven was packed to the brim, almost every table housing tuxedoed boys and dolled-up girls alive with energy.

In the middle of the restaurant, in the same booth they sat in every weekday after school, sat our intrepid troupe of main characters.

"You did *not*," Sarah Farrow said, her mouth agape.

"Oh, I did. After you all left yesterday. Went over to her booth, charmed the fuck out of that weird bitch." Jimbo said, beaming, his pearly-white smile blemished by multiple chunks of beef. "Tonight, Crazy Jane is mine."

Rothschild and Jimbo high-fived, wearing radiant smiles. Jeremy stroked Jenny's thigh under the table in an attempt to keep her cooled down.

"*Groty*, Jimbo. She probably, like, took your hair and made a voodoo doll," Sarah said.

"Hey, if that's what she's into, that's what *I'm* into tonight!" Jimbo shouted.

"Man, tonight's going to be awesome," Rothschild chimed in. He and Jimbo went for another high-five, but this time, Rothschild's elbow hit a water cup on the table and sent it careening all over

Sarah's jeweled dress.

"*Ugh!* You fucking idiots!" She ran, dripping wet and cold, towards the bathroom. Jimbo and Rothschild burst into laughter.

"Aren't you going to go apologize?" Jenny asked Rothschild, venom in her voice. Rothschild coolly took a drink of water.

"Yeah, I think she needs some help," Jimbo said. "Help from your dick!"

Ice water sprayed out of Rothschild's nose and mouth, showering Sarah's meal. He cracked up and held out his hand for yet another high five before turning towards Jenny.

"Yes, your majesty, I *am* going to go apologize. I just had to drink some water first. All this laughing made me thirsty," Rothschild said.

Rothschild got up and walked towards the bathroom. He passed Rachel Severinsen and Corey Jones, who were enjoying their one-hour dinner break from Prom Committee, the first respite they'd received all day. They were making the most of their time off, putting the final touches on their best prank yet: the ruination of Sandy van Thorpe.

Next table over sat Leslie Deakins and Alex Spence, who only stopped smiling and laughing at each other to take bites of their delicious quarter-pounders.

"And then the guy's head gets bigger, and bigger,

and bigger, then *POW!* He explodes into chunks!" Alex laughed. He was telling her about one of his favorite movies to rent from the local video store.

Leslie laughed back. She loved seeing Alex so animated. Watching his excitement made her excited, too.

At the table closest to the bathroom was Matt Brady with his date, a busty, big-haired blonde named Brittany Beverly. The next table over held Sam Berry and Brad Fahey, who kept one eye on their junior-year cheerleader dates and the other on the future prom king and queen.

Rothschild moved past them, towards the bathroom.

"Woah, woah, woah, Rothschild!" Matt yelled. "You going into the girl's room? You so small down there, you forgot you were a man?"

Sam, Brad, and the cheerleaders broke out into identical pangs of laughter.

Back at the table, Jenny's mind fumed. *Why the hell is he friends with these assholes?*

Anxiety seeped into Jeremy's brain. All he wanted was for Jenny's night to be perfect, and that goal was slipping away.

He thought of the answer to her question, the moment he met Rothschild. Jeremy was eight, new to Barbara Falls, stepping into his second-grade classroom for the first time. This is stressful for everyone, but doubly so for a psychic. Jeremy was met with an overload of thoughts, and they were all about him.

New kid, huh? Looks like a loser.

What's up with his eye?

I like pickles.

He looks good at soccer.

The last thought was broadcast from a boy in the back, carrying an air of cool confidence and dressed in a letterman's jacket sized for eight-year-olds. His name was Chris Rothschild. Jeremy sat in the empty seat next to him, and recess soccer sessions cemented their friendship.

Jimbo came along when they were in sixth grade, and they had stuck together ever since. Sure, they could be obnoxious at times, and he didn't really have much in common with them, but they were his best friends.

When you're young, you believe the friends you have are the only ones you will ever have, and even if they aren't your best match, you'll stick by their side.

Jeremy tightened his grip on Jenny's thigh and sent her a knowing, apologetic smile. She forced one back.

In the ladies' room, Sarah was making her way through a forest's worth of paper towels. A shower of expletives left her mouth as she threw pile after pile into the garbage.

Rothschild walked in like he was a regular visitor. "Hey, babe, sorry about that. You need some help drying off?"

Sarah spun towards the door, fury on her face. She chucked a handful of damp paper towels at him, which bounced off his chest and onto the floor.

"Hey, watch it, babe. You're gonna get my suit wet," he said.

Her eyes doubled in size, blood vessels ready to pop in anger. She walked up to Rothschild and slapped him across the face. For a moment, they stared at each other, unblinking.

"Woah," Rothschild said. "That was kind of hot."

"Fuck me. Right here," Sarah said.

"What if somebody..."

Sarah shushed him with her tongue. Content with that answer, he slopped his tongue in and around her mouth and tackled her against the sink. His hands tightened around her as he fumbled with the zipper on her dress.

"Let's shake this burger house to the ground," Sarah said.

"Cool," Rothschild said, always one for words. Sarah's dress fell off, revealing a skimpy, bejeweled bra. She always made sure her *entire* outfit matched.

Rothschild was about ready to take his pants off

when they heard a knock on the bathroom door. A voice seeped in from outside.

"Hey, give it a break in there, Rothschild! Some of us are trying to eat!"

Rothschild sighed. "Matt…"

"*Fucking* Brady," Sarah groaned.

Matt, Sam, Brad, and Beverly snickered loudly as the two exited the ladies' room, Sarah beet-red with embarrassment and Rothschild with anger.

"Good one, Matt!" Sam Berry said.

"Yeah, Matt! You're great!" Brad Fahey said.

"Sorry to interrupt," Matt continued. "But the thought of you two boning almost made me barf!" His cronies erupted with laughter.

Rothschild flipped him off as they walked back to their booth. "I'm gonna kick your ass, Matt."

"As if!" Sam Berry answered.

"You'd have to go through us first!" Brad Fahey continued.

"See you at the dance, guys!" Matt called out to the long-gone couple. "Hope you're there for my Prom King crowning ceremony!"

Rothschild and Sarah returned to their booth. Jimbo was talking to Jeremy and Jenny with excitement.

"You two should totally come over to my place after the dance. I've got a ton of beer, and you can spend the night on my couch. It's a fold-out," he said.

"I mean, we'll probably want some alone time together after the dance," Jeremy said.

"Pssh, gay," Jimbo said. "Just screw in the bathroom real quick like Sarah and Rothschild here."

"That was *not* what we were doing," Sarah said. "There was just, like, a lot of water on me, and it took a long time to dry off."

"Sure, you big slut," Jimbo said.

"You don't think that piece of shit over there is going to be Prom King, do you?" Rothschild asked, pointing at Matt, who was telling his admirers a gripping story about a touchdown he once ran.

"I mean, he's nominated. Somebody voted for him," Jeremy said.

"Oh, please. Sandy van Thorpe is nominated for Prom Queen, and nobody voted for her," Rothschild shot back.

"That loser totally cheated. I mean, she was in charge of the nomination ballots," Sarah said.

"But, okay, look. It's me, Matt, and Sam Berry up for Prom King. Brittany Beverly, Sarah, and Sandy van Dork for Queen. Everybody likes me and Sarah more than Matt and Brittany, right? Like, they're total assholes," Rothschild said.

"Total assholes," Sarah echoed.

"Guess we'll see tonight," Jimbo said.

"Well, one thing's for sure: if Matt Brady wins

Prom King, I'm going to hang myself," Rothschild said. "You have my word."

"Oh, stop being a drama queen," Sarah said. *As if those hands could even tie a noose*, Jeremy heard her think.

"Yeah, it's just a plastic crown," Jenny broke in. Sarah and Rothschild looked at her as if she were expounding the merits of the Nazi Party.

"A plastic crown? *A plastic crown?*" Rothschild asked. "That plastic crown is a metaphor, Jenny. A metaphor that says you made your mark on the town of Barbara Falls."

"Do you know what a metaphor is?" Jenny asked.

"A metaphor that says, no matter what happens to you the rest of your life, you were the single coolest dude in your senior class. The stuff of legend. Your name in the history books."

"But could you even name who won Prom King, say, four years ago?" Jenny asked.

"Richie Montgomery," Rothschild, Jeremy, Sarah, and Jimbo all said in unison.

"Ask us what the square root of 256 is next, Jenny," Jimbo said.

"Dude was so cool," Rothschild said. "And look at him now!" Rothschild swung a hand towards the Hamburger Heaven kitchen, where Richie Montgomery, sporting a red and white manager's uniform, was chastising a fry cook.

"What a legend," Jimbo said.

"Okay, fine, but isn't having a good time more important than winning some popularity contest?" Jenny asked. "You only get one prom."

"You sound like my fucking mom, Jenny," Rothschild said.

Jeremy's calming grip on his girlfriend's leg had now cut off all feeling below her left thigh. Their romantic dinner had been thoroughly pissed on.

At least I haven't seen anybody get murdered today, he thought.

Yet, thought the narrator.

Chapter 7

Mr. Jeffrey Deakins had lied to his daughter. Leslie had made him promise he wouldn't be one of the teacher chaperones at the prom, but as soon as Principal Wiener asked for volunteers at the March staff meeting, his hand shot up.

He trusted Leslie. He really did. He believed he and his wife had done an admirable job raising their only child and that she was a moral, strong young woman who would do the right thing. He was so proud of her, so proud of her performances in the school plays, so proud of her unique outlook on life.

But the last few years had been so hard. Watching his wife wither into a pale specter of herself as the breast cancer ravaged her body for three damn years… and to stand alongside her with their daughter, tears in her eyes, the understanding of life's cruelties marking her cherubic face for the first time. He'd lost a part of himself, a part he still had yet to find.

And then that twerp Alex Spence came around. He believed Leslie would only fall for an impeccable, perfect boy, but there was something off about Alex. His smiles looked forced. His laughs went on for *just* too long. And that mole on his face. Who could trust a boy with a mole?

When Mr. Deakins arrived at the high school, the gymnasium was ready to go. The bleachers were retracted, leaving the entire gym floor for dancing and eating space. Cut-out stars twinkled in the sky, balloons littered the floor, and a spread of snacks, desserts, and punch decorated a long table wrapped in glittery linen. Sandy van Thorpe, whom his daughter had cried many a tear over, ran around like a goat with its head chopped off, perfecting her final touches before doors opened to students in an hour.

It was all so nice. So reminiscent of his own prom, with his soon-to-be wife, his future still unforeseeable, luminescent, awake with possibility. A time when he could feel pure love, unburdened by the knowledge that it would never last. A time when his mind's picture of his wife wasn't from her death bed, her face caved in from chemo.

He knew he was just thinking of excuses not to like the boy. Leslie was his only daughter. She was all he had left.

No little girl should have to attend her mother's

funeral. These days, he was trying to bring joy back into her life, to help her see the sunshine again without the clouds obscuring the view. He knew this boy was going to ruin all his hard work. Young love meant heartbreak. And he couldn't bear to see his little pumpkin cry again.

So, here he was, in the Barbara Falls gymnasium, spending his Friday night watching the kids he tried so desperately to turn on to science get *too* turned on by slow dances. He made his way towards the other teacher chaperones, who stood semi-circled by the snacks, pretzels and punch in their hands. There were five teachers working the event, plus Principal Wiener and Nancy the receptionist.

"I tell you, Cheg Larson walked out of Wiener's office with his tail between his legs! I don't know what the man did in there!" Mrs. Poughkeepsie said as Deakins walked up. Poughkeepsie hated everything about prom, but she worked the event each year to have something to complain about.

"Wiener's gone completely wacko. Man never leaves his office. And when he does, it looks like he hasn't slept in months," said Mr. Stannaker, the handsome, young history teacher in his first year at B.F. High.

Stannaker was already one of the kids' favorites, and it was no wonder with his slicked-back, dark brown hair, his manly, prominent facial features, and his devil-may-care attitude in the classroom. He was dressed to the nines, suit jacket and all. Deakins guessed he would be a popular dancing partner tonight.

"I agree, it's been…" Mr. Doughty, a math teacher who had been at the school since the cavemen roamed, began before getting cut off.

"I love it. He hasn't complained about my lesson plans once this month. Let the dude go wacko! As long as it means there's no Wiener up my ass!" Miss Bernal, the art teacher, jumped in. Bernal was a flower-child who led her art class with a fist made of Play-Doh.

Coach Kumin, the gym teacher, stood indifferently at the edge of the semi-circle, munching on a mountain of chips and pretzels. He was a man of few words, except around his wrestling squad, who he worked to the ground every practice. Those who made a crack about his last name were never the same afterwards.

"What do…" Mr. Doughty said to no one.

"Well, I hope he's got the same furor tonight that he had yesterday with Cheg Larson. Just thinking about the atrocities these teenagers are going to pull gives me the heebie-jeebies," said Mrs. Poughkeepsie.

"Barb, how could you say that? Tonight's the

night all the young love that's been blossoming for months comes to fruition! An amazing spring harvest," mused Miss Bernal.

"Yeah, as long as they protect themselves," Stannaker said. "Not emotionally, of course. Those scars will last a lifetime no matter what they do."

"Devils, all of them! With fiends like Cheg Larson and Jimbo McKinney running around, it's a miracle half these kids aren't bringing their babies to prom!" Poughkeepsie was now shouting, her skin flapping.

Mr. Deakins excused himself from the conversation. He wanted no talk of sexual atrocities, nothing to fan the flame of fear in his gut about his pumpkin.

The gym made up the east side of Barbara Falls High. Its size dwarfed the other rooms in the building, acting as a reminder that playing games with balls is far more meaningful than learning. Exiting the gym spat you out into a large square foyer where kids would hang out in the morning before class. To the left was the front door to the building, to the right the entrance to the front office, and straight ahead a hallway: the gateway to B.F. High's classrooms.

Deakins walked down the long corridor of lockers sporting patchy, faded blue paint jobs. This was one of two long hallways in the school; Mr. Deakins' biology room stood in the one farthest from the front door, next to the cafeteria, which doubled as an auditorium for the school's drama productions.

Mr. Deakins decided to spend some time alone in his classroom. He'd never become close with many of his fellow teachers. Poughkeepsie was an exhausting slog, and, at almost fifty, he felt isolated from the younger staff, like Bernal and Stannaker. The world just moves too fast to keep up.

He shoved his key into the latch of room 132. Over the last seven years, he'd made the room his own. He stared at the poster hanging from the door chronicling the evolution of man and remembered the stir it had caused when he first taped it up.

Deakins entered the darkened classroom and turned on the lights. Posters both scientific and inspirational lined the walls. In the back was the class guinea pig, Truffles. High school biology meant dead frogs on a plate, but he used Truffles to remind the kids the discipline came out of love for the lifeforms inhabiting this wonderful planet.

He sat at his desk and took a deep, lonely sigh. It would be a long night. Maybe he'd made a mistake. He trusted Leslie, didn't he? And what if she was mad about him lying?

Nothing you can do about it now, Dan, he thought.

He sat and enjoyed the silence. Until the silence stopped.

A sudden, pained shrieking burst from the back of the class. He looked towards the wire cage that held the class pet.

"Truffles?" Deakins stood up and walked towards the cage. With each step, the shrieking got louder, as did Deakins' concern. He didn't know a guinea pig could make so much noise.

"What in the hell..." Deakins' face whitened in disbelief as he looked in the cage.

The cage hung wide open, its wire latch burnt to a crisp. The two-pound creature inside had quadrupled in size, inflated like a balloon. Her black-and-brown coat littered the bottom of the cage, a carpet for the now bald, pink rat. Her stomach pulsated, exasperated squeaks coming with each bloat.

Then the squeaking gave out, replaced by whispered choking noises. Truffles' stomach grew larger and larger until it split open completely, sending a spray of gore across Deakins' glasses and into his unfortunately ajar mouth.

"Oh my God!" Deakins screamed, taking the Lord's name in vain like the heathen scientist he was. He gagged and took off his glasses to wipe them on his argyle sweater vest. Blinded, he didn't see the litter of creatures writhing from the cage and falling onto the floor.

He thrust his clean spectacles back on his face and

was met with the wholesome sight of a hollowed guinea pig carcass, rib cage split in two and internal organs strewn across its caged home. Lying in Truffles' corpse bowl was a monstrous little creature, about four inches across, not breathing or moving.

Deakins loved animals and would normally examine a creature like this with a smile on his face and questions in his brain. But all he felt looking at the *thing* in that cage was pure disgust.

The creature was a repugnant shade of yellow-green. It resembled a slug with a large tumor growing from one end. He guessed that growth was its head; it had a small mouth-like gape and a row of horns growing along the top. Abscesses covered its slimy skin and dripped what looked like chunky, yellowed milk.

He couldn't believe the creature he was staring at could be alive anywhere, let alone inside a guinea pig. Lost in thought, he took a step back and brushed his left leg against a chair, feeling a damp warmth against his ankle but not daring to look away from the horror nesting inside his pet.

This warmth soon became a sharp sting, enough to distract him from the sight. He looked down and lifted up the left leg of his slacks.

There were more than just one of those things he saw in Truffles' cage. Because one of them was crawling up his leg.

Deakins screamed and toppled onto the floor, tipping a table and a couple chairs as he fell. The thing was halfway up his leg, almost at the knee.

He began hyperventilating. *Calm down, Deakins,* he thought. *Whatever it is, it's probably harmless.* He stared at the creature.

For a few seconds, it was still. It then perched up on its lower half, like a jump-yipping prairie dog, before its mouth hole opened wide and began depositing a stream of grainy vomit chunks, the consistency of porridge and the color of nuclear waste, onto his leg.

As soon as the substance touched Deakins' leg, he gasped in pain. The porridge bubbled under his skin, seeping through it and fusing with the flesh, leaving a patch of his leg the purple of spoiled meat. The scorching sting lasted for about ten seconds. Then, it felt like he had no limb at all.

The creature let out a miniature screech and dug its toothless head orifice into Deakins' leg. The violaceous flesh the hell porridge touched now had the consistency of gelatin, and the thing chowed down with infant glee. Deakins' leg disappeared into the creature; each bite it swallowed made its slimy, wound-covered torso grow in size.

The feasting was painless for Mr. Deakins, who only felt the odd sensation of no longer having a left leg. Still, the fear never let up. Afraid to touch the hellspawn, he pulled himself towards the toppled desk, next to which lay a heavy biology textbook.

He grasped the book with both hands and torpedoed it down onto his half-leg with a loud splat. Chunks of flesh gelatin flew through the air like a fat child cannonballing into a pool. The creature exploded in a mist of blood, staining the floor with red.

Deakins again remembered to breathe. He sucked in the air and felt it relax him, then looked at his leg, or what was left of it. The foot clung to the rest of his body by strands of tendon, a marionette doll swaying from bloodied strings.

Blood gushed from his leg. He knew he didn't stand a chance if he stayed here.

Besides, he had to get up, to warn someone. Half the school was on their way to the prom, and God-knows-how-many horrible creatures were crawling right towards them!

You can do it, he thought. *Just bounce on the right leg. One step at a time. If you can get through losing Susie, you can get through this.*

He had to make it. For Leslie.

He closed his eyes and took a deep breath. He would get up on three.

"Three… two…"

As he mouthed the word "one," he felt a slimy warmth on his head as a spray of lukewarm porridge choked out his eyesight. His body seized, his brain coagulated. And all went black.

Chapter 8

"Make a straight line and have your tickets ready!"

A small crowd pooled outside the school. Doors opened in five minutes, and Sandy van Thorpe was attempting to enforce order on the increasingly excited gaggle of teens.

"The quicker you make a straight line, the quicker I can get you all into that dance! C'mon, guys, let's act like adults here!" Sandy yelled. She was thoroughly ignored.

"God, look at the controlling little cunt," Rachel Severinsen muttered. She sat inside with Corey, her fellow Prom Committee slave, at a table placed by the gym doors. There, they would check people's tickets and make sure everyone paid the $1 attendance fee.

She couldn't hear what Sandy was saying through the glass doors, but she could guess. *Act like adults* this, *let's go, guys* that. The same bullshit she and Corey had heard for the last two weeks.

"We're gonna get her, babe. Don't worry," said Corey. His suit jacket and slacks clashed with his mud-splattered baseball cap and patchy, black facial hair. Corey was the son of a cemetery groundskeeper, and he was less intelligent than his blank stare and mouth breathing let on.

He held up a paper bag he had hidden under his chair. The snickers Rachel and Corey let out when it was in sight hinted there was something much more dastardly inside than Hamburger Heaven leftovers.

"That bitch is gonna flip," Rachel said. She was Corey's perfect companion: a country gal with attitude, a long frizz of hair that ran down her back, and flamboyant breasts that took up most of her five-foot frame. They both laughed. Nobody could make slaves of Rachel Severinsen and Corey Jones.

Outside, Brittany Beverly, clinging tumorously to Matt Brady, complained while Sandy herded the crowd into a straight line.

"I'm just, like, saying, if that fucking *virgin* Sandy rigged the votes so she wins Queen, I will flip," she said. "She's totally the type of grody bitch to do it, too. Fucking wannabe."

"Babe, I swear to God, there's no way anybody but you and I are going to be prom royalty tonight," Matt Brady responded. "There's nobody hotter or cooler than us."

"You got that right," Sam Berry said.

"You sure do," echoed Brad Ferry. Sam and Brad, arms around their dates, walked inches behind Matt and Brittany, as if they received sustenance from their shadows.

"You *better* be right. I didn't wear a dress and heels to school every day for the past three months to lose to Sarah fucking Farrow," Brittany said.

"You're beautiful, Brittany," Sam Berry's date said.

"And the best head cheerleader ever," echoed Brad Ferry's date. Sam and Brad had been careful not to use their dates' names after Sam switched them up earlier in the night. This would ensure they would *at least* suck their cocks later.

Brittany blushed. "You guys are *so* rad! I'm so glad you came along with us." She tiptoed her seven-inch heels over to Brad and Sam's dates and gave them both hugs and cheek kisses.

Dick Wong-Dick walked behind the squealing girls. He hadn't decided who he would vote for tonight; no one nominated had bothered to talk to him all semester. His orange suit was nearly phosphorescent in the evening sky and would have been a danger to pilots if any planes ever flew over the city.

He noticed many girls were walking in without a date. Good-looking girls at that. He had a chance yet.

Behind him walked Jeremy Vernon and Jenny Hibiscus, hand in hand.

"As soon as we get in there, it's all about us. No more Rothschild. No more Jimbo. Just you and me," Jeremy whispered in Jenny's ear.

She smiled at him. "Yes, please. Was it that obvious I didn't enjoy dinner?"

"Hmm… maybe just a bit," Jeremy chuckled, holding up two fingers spaced far apart. "It's fine, though. I don't think anybody else noticed."

"They were a little busy thinking about themselves," Jenny said. The smile on her face fell away. "Sorry, I'm being a downer."

Jeremy pulled her closer. "You could never get me down with a smile like that."

"Hey, does anybody know what band Sandy van Dweeb hired for tonight?" Rothschild asked from behind them.

"I think they're called The Gentlemen," Jeremy said.

"Yeah. They came all the way from Seneca. Guess Sandy van *Dumb* put some money towards them," said Jimbo.

"Well, they better be good. I'm trying to boogie," Rothschild said, grabbing Sarah by the hips and shaking her left and right. "If this one's ready for me."

"You know I am," Sarah said. They embraced in

a kiss.

"Man, no sight of Crazy Jane yet. Hope that bitch shows up," Jimbo said.

"Even if she does, she'll want, like, nothing to do with you, Jimbo," Sarah said. "And then *you're* going to owe me ten whole dollars."

"That's what you think, you dumb slut," Jimbo said. "She'll show up. She's probably just getting in a quick pre-prom wrist slit." He mimed the action and stuck his tongue out at Sarah.

"Okay, everybody! Listen up!" Sandy van Thorpe screamed from the front steps of the school, a smile football fields wide on her face. "Who's ready to party?"

The raucous response she expected was instead scattered applause. Her smile didn't fade.

"Here we go… 3… 2… 1… happy prom, everybody!" Sandy opened up the doors, and the crowd funneled in towards the gym.

Across the street, a man in a faded trench coat watched the group of teens scream, laugh, and run into the school. He watched in silence, one hand nuzzling the head of a robotic dog, the other clutching a red and black luchador mask.

Nancy rapped on Principal Wiener's office door for the fourth time that evening. His room had been closed and locked all day. There was something very wrong. She had been the receptionist at B.F. High for almost four years and had never gone a full day without seeing Wiener.

Her knocks were again met with silence. She pounded a couple more times.

"Come *on*, Forrest. Everybody's wondering why you're not out there. Kids have entered the building," Nancy said.

The door swung open instantly, as if Wiener had been leaning right against it. His toupee sat sideways, and his five o'clock shadow was approaching two in the morning. His bloodshot eyes bulged from his sockets. Nancy took a step back at the sight of him.

"I told you, Nancy, *don't* call me Forrest. He'll hear you." Wiener took two steps towards Nancy. She took the same steps backwards.

"What are you talking about?" Nancy's heart pumped faster as Wiener inched towards her. "What's wrong? You've been locked in there all day."

"I've been preparing. It's time."

"Yeah... time for prom. Time for you to get out there and cheer on the senior class. Right after you clean yourself up." She continued stepping away from Wiener, her brain sensing danger.

"Oh no. Not yet. They'll understand why... soon." Wiener hadn't blinked since opening the door. Veins popped from his neck like tributaries.

Nancy jumped as something touched her back. A file cabinet. She was out of space to back up. Wiener continued getting closer.

"Principal Wiener, you're scaring me."

"Nancy, this won't be the most scared you'll get tonight," Wiener said, a sly smile wrapping itself across his face. "Not even close."

Nancy swept her head left and right. She needed a weapon, anything to defend herself. She spotted a stapler on her desk and prepared for a mad dash when Wiener, without a word, turned around, walked into his office, and slammed the door behind him.

She took a long, deep breath. Her fear started to subside, but, alone in the darkened office, anxiety remained. Wiener or no Wiener, she was going to the gymnasium.

Nancy, like most, found safety in numbers. She would soon find the only safe place in Barbara Falls tonight was inside your own coffin.

"Oh, oh, *Sheila,* let me love you 'til the morning comes!" Punchy drums and synthesized arpeggios filled the gymnasium. The crowd, building in size, embraced the dance floor in response.

On stage, providing the aural lubrication, were the Gentlemen. Their lead singer wore skin-tight, neon-pink workout clothes, oversized feathered earrings, and enough face makeup to snuff out a mime. Her name was Deborah Moyet, and she danced around the stage like she owned it, trying to forget that this small-town prom was the biggest gig she'd ever played. No, it wasn't Madison Square Garden, but Moyet still yearned to have this crowd in the palm of her studded-gloved hands.

Accompanying her on the makeshift plywood creation B.F. High called a stage was a motley crew of giant, eye-catching coifs of hair and retina-raping apparel. David McCluskey, on lead synth, felt more bitter than Moyet about tonight's gig. He wondered why he was not taken seriously in the musical community, as he performed a modified chicken dance in his black-and-white piano-key suit.

Only a few timid students resisted getting their groove on, instead sitting on the sidelines and chowing down on snacks. Crazy Jane, or, as she preferred, Jane, was one of them. She sat at a table bordering the far wall and languidly sipped a glass of punch. Her long, jet black dress was flanked by a pair of black wedges and black lipstick.

The punch tasted cheap and spiked with grain liquor. Jane couldn't believe she was here; all year, she told herself she'd spend the night alone in her room, listening to *The Firstborn is Dead,* writing poetry, hell, even looking at a wall. Anything better than spending her night with a collection of dimwits dancing to awful music and pretending their meaningless lives were important.

Yet, here she was. Why?

For one, even if the Gentlemen were an amateurish new-wave cover band, they *were* a band, a rarity for the isolated, backwoods Barbara Falls. Jane's plan after graduation was to move to New York City, where she could finally see her idols, bands like the Sisters of Mercy and the Cure, play live. Until then, she would have to settle for the Gentlemen.

And then there was Jimbo McKinney.

Jane found Jimbo revolting. His whale of a head. His stupid voice. His treatment of women. Even looking at his face shrouded her vision in a cloak of revulsion.

Luckily, the oaf's attention usually focused on the buxom blonde bimbos of Barbara Falls. Until yesterday, at Hamburger Heaven. He approached her table. Interrupted her Clan of Xymox album. Asked her what she was listening to, like he had any *idea* about art. Breathed waves of meat stench into her face. And then... flirted with her?!

As he made his vapid attempts to breed with her, Jane formed a thought in her mind. If he wanted her body, she could use that against him. She would cut off Goliath's head in front of the whole school. How? She wasn't sure. All she knew was Jimbo McKinney had flirted up the wrong tree.

As if her mind's hatred summoned him, Jimbo interrupted her thoughts, pulling up a seat next to her and plopping into it like a beached beluga.

"So, not too cool for prom after all, eh?" Jimbo asked. He smiled, showing a set of teeth littered with beef bits.

"No, I am," Jane said blankly. "But, sometimes, it's good to see the view from down here." The line between jest and sincerity barely existed for Jane; she liked to confuse people almost as much as hate them.

"Well, the view from here is pretty great," Jimbo said, looking directly at her chest instead of her eyes, unable to wipe the shit-eating grin off his face. "I think you may have come just to see me."

Jane leaned in. "And did you ever think that might be all in that big head of yours?"

Jimbo thought and thought for a clever response, finally settling on, "Pssh, no, that would be dumb!"

"Funny, dumb is *just* the word I was thinking of," Jane said.

Jimbo did not have the wit to carry on a conversation with a girl of moderate intelligence, and he had the vaguest inkling that Jane was making fun of him. His iron-clad pride and mortiferous sex drive, however, trumped all other feelings. Losing a bet *and* failing to get laid in one night was Jimbo's nightmare fuel.

"Come on, let's dance." Jimbo put his arm out towards Jane.

"To *this*?" The Gentlemen had just started a cover of "Wake Me Up Before You Go-Go," eliciting dance mayhem amongst the students. Drummer Steven Sylvian pounded his kit with one hand, using the other to pound swigs of whiskey from a flask hidden in his clown-print button-up shirt.

"This sounds exactly like what you were listening to yesterday," McKinney said. "Now, stop bitching and start dancing."

Jane took the fuming anger she felt at someone comparing *Medusa* to George Michael and repurposed it into pure dance-floor aggression. She took McKinney's hand, and he pulled her the rest of the way.

"I'm going to tell her she should stay the hell away from Jimbo," Jenny Hibiscus said to Jeremy, who was latched to her hips, lost in an upbeat two-step on the dance floor.

"Jenny, I told you, it's just us tonight. I'm sure Jane has the sense not to sleep with Jimbo without you warning her," Jeremy said, pulling her closer. "Besides, you love this song."

Jenny glanced towards the stage and watched

Deborah Moyet jump up and down while rhyming the words "go-go" and "yo-yo." To her left was the mopey Bernard Hook on bass. Hook had decided playing happy music would help him more efficiently pay his rent, a theory which had so far proven horribly, horribly wrong. Hook shimmied to the left and then the right, a beaming smile on his face and monolithic shame in his heart.

She looked back at Jeremy and smiled. "You're right. I really do."

Who cares about Jane when I have Jeremy? Her thoughts made Jeremy blush, and they continued to two-step. They held each other close, but not intimately enough to draw the ire of Mrs. Poughkeepsie, who kept her hawk eyes on every teen in the gymnasium.

Poughkeepsie was so hell-bent on stopping fornication that she hadn't noticed Mr. Deakins had been gone for over half an hour. His absence went almost entirely unacknowledged: Miss Bernal was in her car enjoying a quick toke, Mr. Stannaker danced with a popular, full-chested junior, and Coach Kumin had almost finished his second bag of pretzel twists. Mr. Doughty had tried to alert all four of them that Deakins was missing, but no one realized he was talking to them.

Nancy the receptionist opened the doors to the gymnasium, gooseflesh invading her body like a case of E. coli. She walked up to Poughkeepsie, who did not notice Nancy's face was the color of a bed sheet.

"Where's Principal Wiener? This is ridiculous, taking on all this promiscuity by myself!" Poughkeepsie complained.

"He's not coming out of his office," Nancy said, her voice drained of feeling. "And I think it's better that way."

Poughkeepsie put down her binoculars, her tool for accurately gauging the number of inches between teen genitals, and looked Nancy in the face.

"You tell that man to get his butt in gear. You know as well as I do that it's the principal who crowns prom royalty. *And* handles discipline! Who else is going to do it? Are *you* going to do it, Nancy? *You?*" Her neck fat began to jiggle.

Nancy shook her head, staring past her with the eyes of a war veteran.

"What's wrong with you, Nancy? Is there a gas leak in that office or something?" This was the closest Poughkeepsie got to feeling concern for her coworkers.

"I think Principal Wiener is really, really sick. And I think we should call the police before he does something horrible." Tears bubbled in Nancy's eyes.

Poughkeepsie's thick, scruffy eyebrows angled to

45 degrees behind her thick-rimmed glasses. She scoffed and brought the binoculars back to her face.

"Well, whatever sick he's got, he passed it right on to you! I swear, everyone's acting kooky around here!"

Nancy felt her fear lessen, distracted by her disdain of Barb Poughkeepsie.

"Besides, you don't need to call the police," Poughkeepsie added. "The entire Sheriff's department is outside the school. It's prom night, silly."

Nancy's eyes brightened. "Oh… you're…"

"Too close!" Poughkeepsie yelled, shuffling from the punch bowl towards an unfortunate dancing couple. Nancy looked to Coach Kumin. He seemed quite content with his pretzels, and she decided some snacks would do her good before a fraught talk with the cops.

Wrapped in Alex Spence's arms, bliss surged through Leslie Deakins' veins. They slow danced despite the upbeat music. Her head against his collar bone, she never wanted to let go.

Alex tried desperately to think away his erection. Alas, the slight brush against a human being with female sex organs was proving too much for him. He hoped Leslie didn't notice.

Leslie, eyes closed and heart content, felt something pull her away from her love. Exiting her kingdom of joy, she lifted her eyelids and was met with a horrifying sight.

"You're dancing too close to each other!" Poughkeepsie squawked, her beet-red neck flaps jiggling in Leslie's face. "Keep it PG! Four inches apart! I won't say it again!"

Poughkeepsie stormed away. Leslie suffered a moment of shellshock. The close-up of Poughkeepsie's neck fat had wholly extinguished Alex's boner.

"Well… okay, then…" Alex said. They stared at each other for a second and burst out laughing. Leslie's cute, dorky chortle lit up Alex's insides.

Alex's family had left Indiana the year before, after Alex came home with a broken arm. A group of bullies had jumped him in the parking lot: his poof of permed hair, drama credentials, and general lack of masculinity made him a favorite target. He thought love was out of his reach, something for normal people, for those better-looking and more sporty than he.

And now, here he was. Leslie was perfect. Her laugh could bring world peace to the Middle East. She had a wit the size of Texas and could own a dramatic role as well as she could a comedic one. She had comfy, cozy, huggable style. And she was here with *him*. He reached out for her hand.

"Careful… four inches between us. I guess you've got to show me your dance moves," Leslie said, swinging Alex's hands like a lovestruck pendulum.

"Sure you can handle it? They're pretty mean," Alex said.

"Not as mean as mine, I betcha." Leslie rocked her hands up and down, leading the two into a skanking jig. Their arms flailed wildly and their legs struggled to keep in time. It was a lovely, pitiful sight.

"I love you, Leslie," Alex said, already out-of-breath from their violent dance.

Leslie's heart burst open in a cavalcade of white doves and red roses. It was the first time he had said those words, and they sounded so, so good.

"I love you too, Alex."

She stood on her tiptoes and they embraced in a kiss. They avoided the gaze of Mrs. Poughkeepsie, as she was busy tearing apart Brad Fahey and his date.

"Wake me *uuuuuuuuuuuuuup!"* Deborah Moyet extended the last note of the life-affirming Wham! track to give time for Sylvian to break out a killer drum fill and guitarist Paul Score to complete the first of his ten nightly "big guitar solos." Sylvian, half a flask of cheap whiskey deep under an hour into the night, barely pulled off his snare roll. Score, who never missed a chance to be the center of attention, moved to the head of the stage, collapsed to his knees, and ran his hands down his guitar in sexual ecstasy.

While Score had a reputation amongst the other Gentlemen as an egotistical dickhead, everyone knew he was the true talent of the group. His solos were legendary. His dress reflected his opinion of himself: a platinum silver jumpsuit, sunglasses with black-and-white hypnotic swirls, and a nine-inch-tall orange haircut fashioned to look like a crab's claw.

After twenty-five more seconds of guitar solo, the band stopped and applause filled the gymnasium.

"Thank you, Barbara Falls High!" Moyet yelled into the mic. "Is everybody having a good night?" *Yes, yes, they were,* said the roar of the crowd.

"We'll be back to the popular hits soon, but first, we're going to play an original song off our new album!"

The raucous clapping fell to a halt.

Paul Score walked to Moyet and pushed the mic stand in his direction. "We've got copies of the album in our van, so come see us after! And call those pricks over at 98.9 KROP-FM and tell them you want to hear *real* music on their station!"

Moyet took the mic back. Score had a habit of calling important people pricks on stage.

"Alright... this song's called 'Let Your Love Fly High,'" Moyet finished. "It's about letting your love spread its wings around those important to you. Hold your lover close."

McCluskey started in with a synth line, then the rest of the band joined in. The song was an upbeat number, and the crowd began to boogie despite not knowing the tune.

"My love is like an eagle / It soars across the sky / Your *lo-oo-o-ve* is like a pigeon / Needs a little help to get by," Moyet crooned.

The youthful love in the room embraced the avian metaphor and spread itself in lush, enveloping brushstrokes across the twinkling stars of the gymnasium. They shined just a bit brighter.

Chapter 9

"Sheriff, I think you're wrong about this whole situation," Officer Robert Briggs said, chewing on a raisin cinnamon roll. The sheriff's wife loaded the police station with goodies each night after closing up her Main Street bakery. Briggs never abstained.

"About the killer?" Sheriff Matthews responded, his eyes fixed on the school. The two were parked in the squad car in the main parking lot, right outside the gymnasium. "I don't know, Briggs, I'm pretty damn sure there's a killer."

"No, no, no, not the killer! No, I sure as heck don't think that guard up at Shady Hills tore *himself* apart from the inside!" Briggs chuckled. "I was talking about you and raisin cinnamon rolls."

Matthews broke his staring contest with the school and narrowed his eyes at Briggs. "What?"

"Couple weeks back, you said you'd rather have cinnamon rolls *without* raisins, and you're just being silly! Your wife's rolls are better with raisins!"

Briggs said.

"Why did you think this was the time to bring this up?"

"Well… is this a bad time?"

"We're trying to find a serial killer."

"While eating cinnamon rolls."

Matthews picked up the patrol car's radio. "Ronnie, anything going on back there? Over."

Officer Ronnie Davidson was parked by the back entrance of the school, over by the auditorium and what was until recently Mr. Deakins' classroom. "Nothing yet, Sheriff. Not even a stray teen. Over."

"Good. Keep me updated," Matthews said. "Over."

"Now, Sheriff, I don't mean to poke, but just yesterday, you was saying how Shady Hills is sure a *loooong* way from Barbara Falls. Yet, here we are, outside the high school looking for this feller," Briggs said. He set the scraps of his cinnamon roll on his paunch of a belly. He never had to do much actual police work in Barbara Falls, and these circumstances were really ruining his appetite.

"I did some research on the escaped prisoner," Matthews responded, his gaze back on the school's entrance. "I didn't like what I read."

"Oh no! You don't mean to say he's a professional dancer? Ready to kill any teen making a mockery of his craft?" Briggs shuddered. "It'd be a bloodbath,

Sheriff!"

"Even worse. He used to be a student here."

"Oh my God... do you think he knows the prom is tonight?" Briggs definitely wasn't finishing his cinnamon roll.

"All I know is..."

Matthews was interrupted by the radio. "Hey, Sheriff, we might have something over here. A male, walking around the back of the school. Over."

The sheriff sat up in his seat and grabbed the radio. "I need more, Davidson."

After a few seconds came the reply: "Oh, you know who it is... it's that damn Pat van Martens kid. Over."

"Pat van Martens. He's a punk-ass, Davidson."

"A punk-ass. Roger that, Sheriff. He's standing by the back door... oh, no, somebody just opened it. Van Martens is walking right in. Over."

"I bet it's Cheg Larson. Another punk-ass, Davidson. That's two punk-asses we're dealing with."

"You want me to go get them?"

"Stay where you are, Davidson. We need both doors covered. Over and out," Matthews said. He turned to Briggs. "Bobby, go through the front, find Van Martens. They're planning something."

"Yes, sir!" Briggs yelled and exited the car, waddling to the front entrance of the school and depositing a trail of cinnamon crumbs on the way.

He was thankful to be chasing two punk-asses and not an escaped serial killer.

Matthews went back to the radio. "Davidson, I sent in Briggs. Anything else?"

He waited ten seconds. Twenty. No response.

"Talk to me, Davidson. Over." Still nothing. "You hear me, Ronnie?"

Damn fool's probably chasing Van Martens instead of manning his post. He decided to go check, just in case. Besides, they needed eyes on the back door.

He made sure his gun, a standard-issue Glock, was loaded, exited the car, and jogged across the front walkway of Barbara Falls High. Rachel Severinsen and Corey Jones sat at a table in the foyer, but they were the only sign of life. No Davidson or Briggs.

A chilled wind gusted through him, and he wished he had brought his jacket along. Instead, all he wore was his officer's uniform. He remembered his father coming home when he was a little boy, dressed in the black and blue, sheriff's badge gleaming on his chest. His father was a great sheriff, and Matthews hoped he was living up to his dad's shining reputation.

The only sound was the muffled play of the band inside. The entrance to the school faced Main Street, but the only business still open on the thoroughfare was Hamburger Heaven down the road. It was dark, too, save for two solitary streetlights flanked by a row of large, dead elm trees, which cast imposing shadows across the sidewalk and parking lot.

It took more than shadows to scare Sheriff Matthews. His colleagues often tried to spook the man, jumping out of closets and leaving prank voicemails on his machine. The games always failed. Fearless Joe Matthews wouldn't crack.

The sheriff walked around the side of the building, scanning left and right across the back lot. Davidson's 4Runner was easy to spot. There were only a few vehicles parked out back, and the beacon on top of the car was switched on, spraying ominous streams of red light into the darkness.

What is that fool doing? Matthews thought.

He walked closer, gun in hand. It looked like something was perched on the windshield, like a turkey. But Barbara Falls *had* no turkeys.

He sprinted to the car and disbelief spread over his face. It was not a bird.

It was Davidson's head, shoved through the windshield from the inside and speared through a section of broken glass. His face had been cut cleanly down the middle, windshield shoved six inches into the bridge of his nose. The car's windshield wiper slapped against the mangled top half of his face every three seconds with a splat.

The flashes of neon light illuminated the scene, then died away. Matted hair covered in shards of glass. Dark crimson blood smeared across the windshield. Ronnie's wide-open, unseeing eyes. There one second, then gone, then there again in a surge of red. A reoccurring nightmare, one impossible to wake from.

Matthews felt remorse for his friend, but knew it did no good to stay and soak in the sights. He turned off the safety on his Glock and ran back to the car, desperate to radio Nancy, to tell her to bring in the Seneca police force, to find a way to stop this bastard. The slam of boots against concrete echoed across Main Street.

Someone was already waiting for him. A large, masked man with a trench coat stood in front of the patrol car. Thick fog rolled across the night air and obscured the man's lower half.

"Put your hands up!" Matthews yelled, pulling his Glock out and pointing it at the man's head. The man did not move.

"Did you hear me? Put your hands above the fog, where I can see them!"

The man calmly raised his right hand, keeping his left hidden. Matthews could see nothing but the outline of his jacket. Where did all this fog come from?

The man stopped moving, his arm parallel to the

ground. He held it there for a few seconds. Then, he flicked his wrist and said a single word.

"Fetch!"

Matthews heard a growl. A dog, maybe, but strangely mechanic, like a canine protecting its family from the sounds of a Macintosh computer.

A second later, an animal sprinted at him out of the fog. And fast, like it was gliding upon the earth. Matthews was thirty feet from the man and knew he had very little time before the dog was upon him. He sprinted towards the closest elm, hoping to scramble up and get a clean shot off at the animal before it was too late.

For the first time in his life, Matthews felt real fear. A voicemail from someone claiming to be Satan was nothing compared to this: true, unadulterated terror. He felt his bladder loosen and his heart rattle in his chest.

Matthews had taken three strides before he felt the wind being knocked out of him from behind. The dog tackled him onto the sidewalk, crushing two of his ribs and skidding his handsome face against concrete.

Pinned to the pavement, the sheriff spit out a mouthful of bloody teeth and tried to pull himself onto his stomach. It was no use. He could barely move under the weight of the creature.

Twisting his head, he finally got a look at his

pursuer. It was no mere dog. Its metal skin shone in the streetlamp glow, and a pair of red eyes promised him this was no prank. Nay, Satan was *here*, and He had cast-iron teeth.

The creature bared those teeth and dug them into Matthews' lower back. The pain was nothing compared to the fear, which had overtaken his being completely. Tears welled up in his eyes, shit rained down his pant legs, and his pulsating heart hammered against the pavement.

Until it didn't. The dog clamped its teeth firmly around Matthews' lower spine and shook back and forth like a puppy with a chew toy. The inhuman incisors wrenched the sheriff's spine from his body, collapsing his jawbone and sending a shower of internal organs across the concrete.

By the front door of the school, a plate's worth of pretzels scattered across the sidewalk.

After eating snacks with Coach Kumin and watching the Gentlemen play, Nancy had finally felt better about leaving the school to talk to the police. Upon stepping outside, though, she was met with the lovely sight of the town sheriff getting his spine ripped out.

Nancy felt the world slip out from under her, her mind free-falling alongside the skittering pretzels. She looked past the sheriff's body. There stood the outline of a masked figure, staring at her through a thick swath of fog.

No. It can't be. She closed her eyes, looked again. The man was gone.

She was dreaming. She had to be. All of tonight, from the confrontation with Principal Wiener to this dog tearing strips of flesh from the sheriff's back. Just one long, terrible dream. She was right now lying down in her bed, twisting and turning in fright, but safe and warm, wrapped in her electric blanket.

Most of us meat sacks aren't brave enough to face death head-on. Faced with the inevitable, we collapse, whining, pleading for moments more of pitiful existence. We waste our lives, and then we waste our deaths.

Nancy was no exception. She was swept into a dissociative state, protected from fear by the cool electric heat of her favorite blanket. Reality far away, she thought nothing of the noose creeping towards her from the roof of the building until it slipped around her neck.

When she was younger, she had once ridden a theme park ride, the Pillar of Doom, that pulled her towards the clouds before dropping her in free-fall back down to the ground. And here she was, back on the ride!

What fun, she thought. *But this seatbelt is so tight... I can barely breathe!*

She tried to choke out a breath as the noose grew tighter and tighter around her throat. The vision of Sheriff Matthews began to tunnel, as blood vessels popped in her eyes and the rope chafed her neck raw.

Please... let me off the ride! she thought, before coughing out her last earthly breath.

Her aquatic-themed word search remains unfinished to this day.

Chapter 10

Corey Jones was too busy fingering Rachel underneath the ticket table to notice the hanging receptionist outside, or even that they had let Pat van Martens and Cheg Larson into the gym without tickets.

Inside, Cheg and Pat crouched under the snack tables, careful to avoid the eyes of the teacher chaperones.

It wasn't difficult. Poughkeepsie's binoculars pointed to the dance floor and nowhere else. Stannaker kept the gaze of a doting senior girl as they slowly jigged to Yazoo's "Only You." Doughty saw them hiding, but didn't want to handle the confrontation. Kumin was eating pretzels and Bernal was bleeding out in her car, her throat slit ear to ear.

"First things first, add a little *punch* to that punch," Van Martens laughed from underneath the snack table. He pulled a fifth of vodka from his leather jacket.

"Those fuckers won't know what hit them," Cheg replied. In fact, they would be the third people to add liquor to the punch, which now tasted more like rubbing alcohol than "Merry Cherry Berry."

Van Martens and Cheg each took a swig and dumped the remainder into the punch bowl.

"Next, the brownies." Van Martens pulled a large bowl of brownies from his leather jacket. The special ingredient: four bottles of extra-strength laxatives mixed into the batter.

They dumped the treats into an empty bowl of chips and high-fived. This indeed would've been a great prank, except that the laxatives took twelve hours to kick in and everyone who ate one would be brutally murdered long before then.

"And, lastly, the music." Van Martens pulled two briefcases of cassette tapes from his leather jacket. "*The Legacy*? *W.A.S.P.*? *Spreading the Disease*? Pick your poison, motherfucker. But don't you dare pick Poison."

Cheg flipped through the cassettes and held up Kreator's *Pleasure to Kill* with a smug smile.

"But how are we supposed to get it over the loudspeakers?" Cheg asked.

"Alright, everybody, it's time for us to take a quick break," Deborah Moyet announced from the stage. "Our amazing sound guy will be playing some choice tunes for you all to freak to while we're gone. Be back in fifteen!"

She blew the audience kisses as the band walked off. The audience lit up in applause. No one clapped louder than Dick Wong-Dick.

Dick was in love. He had never seen a more beautiful woman than Deborah Moyet. Her peacock-feather earrings. Her tight outfit and cat's-eye makeup. Her powerful, booming voice. She was perfect.

Who cared about all these Barbara Falls High girls? The ones who called him Chinese and couldn't understand a word he said? This was a *real* woman, and Wong-Dick knew she was the one for him. He ran out of the gym to follow the band to their van.

"Now's our chance!" Van Martens said. He grabbed the Exodus tape and slunk towards the PA system, set up near the double-door gym entrance.

As he approached the PA, Officer Briggs barreled through the double doors. He let out a huge smile when he saw Pat.

"Got you now, Van Martens," Briggs said as he crossed his arms. "I'm gonna have to take you down to the station."

"Fuck you, pig," said Van Martens. "I didn't do *shit.*"

"Got you on four charges of being a punk-ass. Come with me."

"Eat dick."

"Oh, you'll pay for that one, Van Martens. Get over..."

Before Briggs could get out his sentence, a latecomer to the dance opened the swinging gym doors behind him, catching him in the back and shoving him towards Van Martens. Pat saw it coming and sidestepped. He stuck his foot out and caught the top-heavy cop in the shin.

Briggs fell to the floor with a thunderous thud. Pat ran out the gym doors, almost knocking down the couple entering the gym.

"Fuck you, five-o! Eat some more donuts while you're down there, piggy!" Pat laughed and ran out into the night.

"Good one, Pat," Cheg whispered, still crouching under the snack table. Pat was the best. He had never let him down by growing up, giving in to the man, or accomplishing anything with his life.

"What are you doing down there, Cheg?" a voice came from above.

Cheg looked up to see Coach Kumin, staring down at him while chewing on one of the laxative-laced brownies. Cheg stood up and snickered.

"Nothing, Coach. How's the food?"

"It's free, Cheg. The food is free."

"Oh, yeah? Well... so is *this!*" Cheg raised up his middle finger and waved it in Coach Kumin's face before running away into the dancing area. Coach watched him go and ate another bite.

After two minutes, Officer Briggs had escaped his fate as a downed roly-poly. He was ready to chase after Van Martens when he was stopped by a squawking Poughkeepsie.

"Officer Briggs! I need back-up in here! These kids are practically *lovemaking* right here on the dance floor!" she clucked.

"Mrs. Poughkeepsie, ma'am, that's not really my job... I'm on important business from Sheriff Matthews," Briggs stuttered.

"I don't care if you're catching the Night Stalker! We need to pound some morals into this town's children! One minute, they're having intercourse before marriage. The next, they'll be kidnapping babies for their sexual playpens!"

Briggs knew there was no stopping Poughkeepsie when her neck started flapping. She dragged him by the arm to the snack table, before he had finished saying that he would help her.

"Let's just do it... right here, right now," Rothschild whispered into Sarah Farrow's ear. They were wrapped close around each other on the dance floor, "If You Leave" playing over the loudspeakers.

"Chris," Sarah giggled. "Somebody would totally see us."

"Yeah, and they'd get hot watching us," Rothschild said.

"I mean… who wouldn't?" Sarah laughed. She took her right hand off Rothschild's shoulder and wrapped it around his manhood.

"Awh, Sarah, you're the best," Rothschild moaned.

Cheg ran through the dance floor and bumped Sarah hard into her man. Instinctively, her hand tightened, crushing Rothschild's balls. His face turned blue.

"Mosh pit, motherfuckers!" Cheg said, holding up the devil's horns at them.

"I'm going to kill that guy," Rothschild squeaked out.

"Oh, take a chill pill, Rothschild. This is my favorite song!" Sarah grabbed Rothschild's slumped shoulders and led him in a doubled-over dance. Cheg skanked by himself with a smile, hoping Pat would come back soon.

Pat couldn't believe how great his luck was, what with Officer *Dumb* getting knocked over at the perfect time. He ran to his beat-up red '69 Ford Falcon Coupe, swung open the front door and thrust the keys into the ignition. The sweet sounds of Stormtroopers of Death burst from his cassette deck and into the parking lot.

"He'll put gas on your kids, then throw them

a match... he'll back the car over grandma, then dissect her cat!" Pat yelled as he peeled out of the parking lot, flashing the bird to the pork-wagon parked in the back. He didn't notice Officer Davidson was his favorite kind of cop... a dead one.

Pat hadn't planned on being kicked out of the prom so early. It was barely nine, and he had nothing to do! Stupid cops. He decided to drive to the cemetery, smoke some weed, and piss on a few graves.

He chuckled at a job well-done. Barbara Falls would really be knocked on their ass tomorrow, when they were all hungover *and* shitting themselves. Pat cackled and lit a cigarette before throwing it out the window into a pile of leaves.

The heavy metal pounding from his stereo drowned out the whirring of a pneumatic drill coming from the back seat.

A tearing sensation racked through Pat's spine. He screamed in pain and looked down at his stomach to see a drill tip punch through his belly. A flap of intestine was speared on its end, spinning around like a hellish carousel. His scream was silenced by a strong hand clasping his mouth and pushing him further back into the seat.

"Is this metal enough for you?" the attacker screamed into his ear.

The drill filleted his chest. Pat felt the tool work

his way up through his stomach and into his rib bones. The drill began to grind his bottom ribs into calcific dust.

No, he thought. *Fuck death.*

An intensity ran through Pat's soul. The violence and pain he loved in his heavy metal music was for others, the meaningless idiots around him, not for Pat van Martens. He would live to see tomorrow.

He had just enough strength to pull a switchblade from his jeans pocket. He flipped it open and stabbed blindly towards the back seat. The knife sunk into flesh, and his attacker cried out in pain. The drill loosened and pulled out of his chest completely. A fresh splash of blood splattered his pants and warmed his car seat.

Pat felt his vision narrowing. The thrash metal faded from his ears. As his attacker opened the back door and barrel-rolled onto the street, the world started to fade to black for Pat van Martens.

He knew he needed to get to Barbara Falls Medical Center fast or he would be roadkill. He viewed hospitals as a government tool for drugging the masses into oblivion, but anti-capitalist opinions tend to fall away when a pneumatic drill has just fucked your insides.

He couldn't see shit, though. He was feeling lightheaded and a thick arterial spray of blood was jetting out of his chest right onto his windshield.

The stream of red soon covered his entire field of vision, his wipers powerless against the blood rain coming from inside the car.

The Ford Falcon swerved back and forth down Main Street. A Barbara Falls police officer would've pulled Pat over for drunk driving if any of them were alive enough to be on traffic duty.

Pat reached for the window crank, so he could see anything in front of him. But each crank was a marathon of excruciating pain, and he had to stop after three to avoid passing out.

The window was barely cracked. He was done for.

There was no escape from the creeping death. Pat moaned and laid his head back against his seat. And the music faded out for the last time.

"Oh, *yeah.* You're so fucking crazy."

Jimbo McKinney had lured Jane back to his van, a nine-passenger vehicle with all of its back seats ripped out, making room for a grungy patch of carpet, covered in burn marks and cum stains. The whole van smelled like a whorish, chain-smoking grandmother's musty sweater.

So far, so good, Jimbo, Jimbo thought to himself. His bodacious dance moves in the gym had so charmed Crazy Jane that *she* was the one who suggested they go somewhere with a bit more privacy. And now here they were, in the Love Machine.

Classic bitches, he thought. *Even the craziest of 'em can't resist a hunk of Jimbo.*

He was ready to give Jane the most romantic screw a McKinney could give. She was laying down in the back of the van, propped up against a yellowed pillow with no pillowcase. The Love Machine breathed romance: a single lamp with harsh LED light shined right in Jane's face, and the B-side of Bon Jovi's *Slippery When Wet* played for sensual atmosphere.

He hovered over her, a lion ready to pounce. A lion with the dick of a god.

Jane wondered if the shag carpet underneath her was made of ants. It seemed to be the only way it could itch so badly while she was still fully clothed.

She stopped scratching and looked at Jimbo. It took all her strength to feign a look of barely bridled lust instead of bursting out in laughter. She had told him to take his shirt off, and he obliged after a minute of maneuvering the tight button-up off his swollen chest. Now, he knelt on top of her, looking proud despite obviously never skipping a day of swallowing fifteen or more hamburgers.

"Alright, baby, your turn," Jimbo said with the passion of a washing machine.

Not a chance, Jane thought. "I want to see *all* of you, Jimbo. You take your pants off, and I won't be able to keep mine on for a *second.*"

"Well, if the lady insists." Jimbo smiled and whipped off his belt.

As he undressed, Jane held back laughter at the stained extra-extra-large boxers in front of her. "And those sexy underwear, too, while you're at it."

Jimbo couldn't wait to see the look on that stupid bitch Sarah's face when he told her about this. He slipped off his boxers and let his gargantuan ball python out of its cage.

"Let's go! Time to get back on stage!" On the other side of the parking lot, Paul Score yelled to his bandmates. They had been allotted two fifteen-minute breaks during their set, and they'd already gone over time on their first.

The other Gentlemen crowded around their van, cigarettes in hand, selling merch to no one.

"When will this shit be over? Fucking embarrassing, that's what this is," synth player McCluskey said, sucking on his third straight cigarette.

"What are you talking about? They love us in there! This is the best reception we've ever got," Deborah Moyet said.

"Yeah, playing a bunch of covers! At a senior

prom in fucking Barbara Falls! I've never even heard of this place," McCluskey said.

"Gig's a gig. Hurry up, we're on stage *now*," Score said and walked to the school's back door, accompanied by Hook and Sylvian, who could barely walk there in a straight line.

"Start without me. I just lit this fag," McCluskey responded. The Gentlemen often talked in British slang to emulate their favorite bands from across the pond.

"Fuck you, McCluskey," Score yelled as he walked into the school.

Deborah took one last drag on her cigarette and extinguished it on the ground with her cherry red Dr. Martens. She looked up and saw a young man running towards her.

It was Dick Wong-Dick. Sylvian, Score, and Hook disappeared in the back door, leaving Deborah and McCluskey with the teen. McCluskey knew instantly it was another silly kid hoping to get some from Deborah. He turned away, wondering why no one ever wanted to sleep with the synth player.

"Hi! Wow! Your band is great! Thank you for coming!" Wong-Dick said in perfect English.

Deborah had no idea what this strange young man in the vomit-orange button-up was saying to her. The slight Korean lilt of Wong-Dick's voice thoroughly stumped her Midwestern brain.

"Thank you... my name's Deborah." Deborah held out her hand, making sure to speak really slowly so the foreign boy could understand. She was always polite to fans, even though she could often guess their true intentions.

"Nice to meet you, Deborah. I'm Dick. I love your band!"

Deborah deciphered the message. "I mean, I'm sure the guys would love massages, but it's time to go on stage!"

"What? No..." Dick said, deflated. He thought someone from outside this shitty, podunk town would be different, but it seemed all Americans were the same.

Deborah looked at Dick, who was now looking down at the ground, defeated. *He's bowing at me,* she thought. *How nice.*

She was about to walk into the school, until she remembered something. *Live at Budokan.* She owned the Cheap Trick record when she was a teen, and the story stuck with her: a band struggling in America gets huge in Japan, plays sold-out shows there, and then breaks through worldwide right after. As she watched Dick start to sob in front of her, she had an idea.

"So... where are you from, Dick?" she asked in slow motion.

Dick looked up. "Seoul. Do you know Seoul?"

Deborah's insides fluttered. So-Wu was the capital of Japan! "And how much longer will you be in America?"

"Just one more month."

It's fate, Deborah thought. All she had to do was swoon this Japanese kid, and the Gentlemen would finally get the success they deserved!

"I'll tell you what, Dick, I think you're pretty cute," Deborah lied. "I have to go play a second set, but afterwards, we should talk."

Dick's eyes lit up. " !"

Deborah blew him a kiss and walked inside the school. Manipulating the little doofus was mean, but success always came with a price tag. She'd give Dick a little smooch, and the next thing she knew, she'd be playing Japanese arena shows in his hometown of Soju.

McCluskey watched as Wong-Dick two-stepped in happiness by the back door. He stomped out his cigarette and yelled, "Be happy now, kid! One day, you'll be 27, hoping the cigarettes kill you before the depression!"

"Let's do it on the hood of your car!"

Crazy Jane was running out of options. Taking down Jimbo meant getting him out of his van, but since he'd taken his clothes off, the man was a grunting, humping zombie, flopping on top of her, seemingly hoping the power of his penis would thrust her clothes right off her. A new tactic was necessary.

"Wait, what?" Jimbo said. The spell of all-encompassing horniness lessened for a second and the faculty of human speech returned.

"The hood of your car. It'll be sexy," Jane replied.

"It'll be cold. C'mon, babe, my van is sexy enough."

"What are you… a pussy?" Jane asked with fire.

Jimbo sprung into action at the slightest slight at his masculinity. He jumped to the back doors of the van and swung them open without abandon. He stepped into the night air, dick swinging in the wind.

"M'lady," Jimbo motioned to Jane to get out of the car. "Time to fuck."

"Time to fuck yourself," Jane replied. She leapt forward and slammed the back doors of the van shut in Jimbo's face. He stumbled backwards, nearly tripping on the concrete. Jane latched the back doors and crawled to the front of the van to make sure every door was locked.

Jimbo slammed on the back doors of the van. "What the fuck are you doing, you crazy bitch?!" he yelled. Jane ignored him and scooped up Jimbo's black dress pants, rifling through his pockets.

Got 'em. Jane held up the car keys, smiling at how easy this all was.

Jimbo ran to the front of the van, tugging on the driver-side door handle and swimming in a pool of expletives. Jane crawled back to the driver's seat, slipped the keys in the ignition, and flipped Jimbo off as she put the van into drive and took off into the night.

The van peeled off, leaving Jimbo alone in the dark night. The crisp April air sent a shiver through his exposed buttocks.

Laughter broke out from the other side of the parking lot. He looked over and saw a man in an all-over piano-print suit cracking up at his misfortune. His ball python hung in dismay, now a flaccid garden snake.

What could he do? He couldn't walk home; his house was miles away. A vision of his balls freezing off ran through his head. *No way.*

There was only one option: the locker room. He had an extra change of clothes in his locker. The only problem... the locker room was in the gym.

He ran to the back door of the school and tried to pull it open. Locked. If he went through the front door, he would have to cross the entire prom to get there. The entire school. Including Sarah, who would *know* Crazy Jane left him out to dry.

Still, it was his only option. Everyone was busy

dancing. Maybe no one would notice a naked linebacker streaking across the prom. He ran to the front doors.

By the band van, McCluskey chuckled at the big, fat naked boy abandoned by his girlfriend. *Serves you right,* he thought. *Life's not fair. I should be playing Top of the Pops, not the front of a prom.*

He figured it was time to go back inside. He shut the doors to the van and started to walk back to the school when he stopped in horror.

Standing in his way was a disgusting creature, about two feet high, bubbling, wheezing in pain, and worming its way towards him. It looked like a slug weaned on nuclear waste. A trail of goo followed behind it, and the mere sight of the thing made his stomach leap in revulsion.

"What in the flying fuck…" McCluskey said as the creature's head slowly unfurled. Strands of yellow pus stretched and popped like bubbles from monstrous chewing gum. Its head opened up, revealing what looked like a diseased, syphilitic vagina. McCluskey stared in disgusted awe, until the sickly, unveiled wound shot forth a wad of chunky, yellow vomit, which splattered him right in the stomach.

McCluskey's nausea soon became unimaginable pain. The vomit burnt clean through his piano-key suit and started boiling the skin on his stomach.

McCluskey let loose an off-key scream that made it clear why he was not the band's lead singer.

The conflagration of pain led to abject fear, a need to escape this carnival of horror. McCluskey turned to run from the awful creature, unaware the hellish liquid had soaked through his digestive system and turned his abdomen into delicate gelatin. His spinal rotation tore his gelatinous midsection cleanly in half.

Numb from the waist down, McCluskey didn't know he was tearing himself apart until his top half was plummeting to the ground. He looked back towards the creature in confusion and saw his legs still standing upright, fountains of spurting blood dyeing his black-and-white pants.

The creature sprayed an ocean of vomit chunks onto his lower half and surrounded the fashionable shanks from all sides, oozing around them and swallowing them whole. McCluskey, half from shock and half from liquefying organs, slipped out of consciousness.

His fainting was a rare win in a life full of disenchantment and letdown. McCluskey died blissfully unaware of the creature enveloping his piano-clad chest, his gel-coiffed hair, his nicotine-stained internal organs. He escaped the fate of many and slipped into mortality with nary an ounce of apprehension, being gifted early entry into the eternal void of vacuity.

Chapter 11

"Nice ass, Jimbo!" Corey Jones laughed as Jimbo thrust open the gym doors, one hand cupped around his manhood.

Jimbo bolted through the gym, eyes glued on the far side of the room, where the doors to his locker and his self-dignity stood.

He thought back to running suicides during football practice. *I've got this... I'm probably running so fast, they can't even see I'm naked.*

They could. The second Jimbo burst into the gymnasium with desperate fear in his eyes and wiener in his hands, half the prom dropped their romantic jigs and their jaws at the sight.

He was almost there. Fifty yards. He forced himself to run even faster.

One person in the gym who didn't notice Jimbo was Mrs. Poughkeepsie, her tightly-fastened binoculars obscuring her peripheral vision. Her spectacles were pointed towards Sarah Farrow and Chris Rothschild, and she took a couple steps backwards to more clearly tell if they were breaking her stone-set rules.

Jimbo had no chance. Poughkeepsie moved right in front of him, and with the power of a speeding pickup truck, Jimbo plowed into her, pushed her straight to the ground, and slid two feet on the gym floor before the entwined duo came to a very awkward stop.

Poughkeepsie, now binocular-free, opened her eyes to Jimbo's naked body on top of her. From her throat escaped the loudest, most avian squawk ever let loose on land. Anyone at the dance who hadn't yet noticed McKinney's naked mile turned to see the best tackle the linebacker had ever made.

After two interminable seconds of silence, every teen, adult, and man-child musician in the gym burst into collective laughter. Tears fell from Rothschild's all-American face. Matt Brady collapsed into an apoplectic giggle fit. Even Coach Kumin stopped chewing pretzels and had himself a nice chuckle.

Jimbo tried desperately to get off of the English teacher, but her savage squirming, slapping and squawking kept knocking him back down on top of her. The laughter reached a fever pitch.

It was a moment of supreme joy and lifelong trauma. Luckily, it's hard to develop PTSD when you have under an hour to live.

A smile rarely appeared on Crazy Jane's lipsticked mouth, nor was laughter often released from her smoky throat. Tonight was a wonderful exception.

She'd watched her masterwork unfold from nearby, then driven to Hamburger Heaven to get a strawberry milkshake. She left the van there, keys in the ignition; if a vagrant needed a new Love Machine, today was their lucky day. She now walked back to her home, only half a mile from the high school.

A perfect prom. And to think I almost didn't go. As she walked by the school, her mind flashed towards the future. In one month, she'd be free of this hellhole, downing snakebites in an East Village dive.

Movement from the corner of her eye brought her back to the present. Someone was walking towards her from the school. Her brain said to keep moving, but her body wouldn't listen. The ambling figure came closer, then entered the fluorescent glow of a streetlight.

She realized this someone wasn't a someone at all. It was a... *something.*

A pus-yellow monstrosity, a throbbing, pustular girth of gooey, inhuman psoriasis, taller than she was, and lurching right towards her. From the slimy trail behind it rose wisps of steam, its mucus melting the concrete underneath.

Jane had no idea what she was looking at, but she damn well knew she didn't want to find out.

Still, her body was frozen, her mind paralyzed. She watched the grotesque thing move towards her. It was all she could do.

She then noticed the living tumor was not heading for her, but instead towards a crumpled pile of garbage nestled under a tree. She squinted to see the trash more closely.

It was the town's sheriff. Or what remained of him. His sallow face was fossilized in immortal pain, his body now a heap of innards, a tipped pot of Sloppy Joe meat from the school's infernal cafeteria.

Jane pressed her hands against her mouth. A rush of hot bile climbed up her throat as she watched the creature spray chunks of slimy, mealy rot on Sheriff Matthews' corpse.

The creature's vomit turned Matthews' body a brownish gray, the color of overcooked veal. It approached and contorted its viscous mass around the clump of cop corpse.

After wrapping itself around the sheriff, the lumpy being recoiled, squeaking like a hamster being picked up against its will. The creature must not have thought the dead hunk of pig very appetizing.

Maybe it only liked live meat. And its only

option... was her.

Reality snapped back to Jane, her paralysis gone in a flash. She bolted for the front door of the school. Who knew if more creatures awaited her on the darkened path back to her home? Inside, at least she wasn't alone.

The creature was terrifying, but it wasn't fast. She made it to the front door without a problem, swung open the door, and froze in the front lobby.

Corey Jones and Rachel Severinsen stared at Jane, who stood at the foot of the foyer, eyes wide and pose crouched. Her clothes were ruffled and her eyes suggested she was very, very not okay.

Seconds passed. Corey broke the silence.

"What the fuck is wrong with you?"

Jane took a breath. Based on the condition of its sheriff, she ascertained the Barbara Falls Police Dept. did not have much of a handle on this situation, so she grasped for the next most competent adult.

"Where's Principal Wiener?" she yelled.

Rachel shrugged. "We haven't seen him all night. Probably in his office."

"Lock that fucking door!" Jane pointed at the front entrance and ran the length of the foyer into the school's office. Corey looked at Rachel and laughed.

"Good ol' Crazy Jane! Couldn't think of a better

name for her if I tried!" Corey snorted, forgetting that he never tried at anything.

Rachel laughed, then looked at her watch.

"9:30… half an hour until the royalty ceremony. Half an hour until we take Sandy van Thorpe down to loser town," Rachel said. Overwhelmed by primal urges and thoughts of revenge, the couple embraced and exchanged tongues.

Neither of them noticed the gooey acid-chowder creature moving past the front door, vacantly circling the building for fresh meat.

Jane pounded and pounded on Principal Wiener's door. Getting no response, she finally looked behind her to see if she had been trailed. It looked like she was safe… for now.

"Principal Wiener, please open up! Something horrible is going on outside! Absolutely *horrible*!" she yelled.

Wiener swung open the door with such force that Jane almost fell into his arms. His toupee stuck straight up, barely in contact with his bald head.

"I know," Wiener said. He turned towards his desk, leaving his door wide open. Jane followed him.

"What do you mean, you know?! We have to do something! The Sheriff is a pile of guts outside!"

"Shut the door, Jane."

Jane did as she was told. She tottered towards Wiener's desk.

"Do you know what that... *thing* is out there?" she asked.

Wiener stared out the window. "Yes. Yes, I do."

His voice was cold, strange. She looked down at his desk and saw a manila file. On the front, written in scraggly, thick red, was one word: "KILLER."

"I suppose you want the story," Wiener continued. "It's one I haven't told in ten years. I never thought I'd reveal its secrets to one of my... less memorable students."

Jane was too scared to process his insult. "Tell me what that thing outside is."

"It's my son," said Wiener.

A shiver of guttural fear racked Jane's body. What kind of awful being had Wiener impregnated to birth the monster outside?

"The year was 1977. Jimmy Carter was the president, the war in Vietnam was over, and I was a father."

Principal Wiener felt the present day melt away. He saw a younger Wiener, hair on his head and love coursing through his veins, sitting at his kitchen table. To his left, his beautiful wife, to his right, his son, 10 years of age, blonde bowl-cut and wide-rimmed glasses on his face.

"Benjamin was everything I could ask for. He

obeyed his parents, did well in school. There was no doubt he would go on to great things.

"It was my fifth year here as principal when Benjamin entered high school. Before then, I thought little Benny's life was perfect. Every parent does. But watching the way the kids treated him... picked on him... it tore me up inside."

"Get out of the way, Wiener!" A flashback of a leather-clad boy pushed Benjamin into his open locker. Benjamin, now an acne-covered senior with long, unkempt blonde hair, crumpled against it, spilling his books and papers everywhere. The greaser laughed and high-fived his friend. Wiener watched his younger self help Benjamin up, gather his things, and storm off in search of those who dared touch his son. Along the way, he shed a single tear.

"Benny changed. He was more brooding. Withdrawn. He snapped at me and my wife. Every day after school, he would go upstairs, lock himself in his room, and listen to that awful devil's music of his."

Flashback Wiener stood outside a locked bedroom, ear pressed against the door. The sound of violin, *guitarrón*, and trumpet reverberated across his face. He turned and shed two single tears.

"Mariachi. That damned mariachi. It never stopped. And always the same record."

In the present day, Wiener opened his manila file and took out a scan of album art, holding it up for Jane to see. *El Cazador's Mariachi de Luchador*. Pictured were seven men holding acoustic guitars, trumpets, and other instruments in front of a Catholic church. It could've been any album from America's downstairs neighbor, save for their outfits: the band was dressed as luchador wrestlers, tight red, blue and green masks on their face, shirtless with tights and knee-high black boots.

"It was all he did. Just sit in his room all day, transfixed by the sounds. Still... harmless, right? That's what I thought until I played the record backwards."

Wiener sat on Benjamin's old bed, many a single tear rolling from his face. Coming from the stereo was a string of messages.

God is dead.

Satan is the answer.

Liberate the Earth of scum.

"The pleasant Mexican music was a cover-up for some... devil-worshipping cult. My son was brainwashed, and he didn't even know it! I burned the record. I banned mariachi from the house. I took away his record player.

"And then prom came."

Wiener stood in the gymnasium, the same one The Gentlemen currently waited in for their synth player. A group of 1970s teenagers danced around, calling each other "groovy" and playing with lava lamps. Disco blasted from speakers, and the dance floor was sick with Saturday night fever.

"Everyone was there, except for my son. He was sitting at home alone... or so I thought. Until a colleague told me about a different dance happening that same night..."

"Concert? What concert?" Flashback Wiener asked the teacher next to him.

"Oh, some mariachi band playing the arts center at the edge of town. It's a shame, I thought we did a pretty good job keeping those browns out of Barbara Falls," said the man.

Wiener's eyes grew wide. "Did you say mariachi?"

"Yeah, you know," said the man, going into a rendition of Johnny Cash's "Ring of Fire," making him the second most knowledgeable person on mariachi in the room.

Wiener didn't hear his impression. He was running to the nearest phone.

"Honey, tell me..." Wiener said as the calming voice of his wife came over the receiver. "Is Benny home?"

"Of course, Forrest. He's right here on the couch watching *Nashville 99* with me. I'm staring at him right now!" she said.

Relief rained over Wiener. "Oh, thank God. Honey, I just heard..."

"*Oh my god, Forrest!* This isn't Benjamin at all! It's a *mannequin* wrapped in *blankets!*"

"No... no..."

"He's gone, Forrest! *He's gone!*"

He left his wife screaming on the line and ran to his car. Then, he heard them. Motorcycles revving down Main Street.

A group of bikes was coming right for the school. Riding them were masked men, capes flapping in the wind behind them. The cold splash of fear filled Wiener when he saw their outfits. Tights. Knee-high black boots. And luchador masks.

The gang stopped on the sidewalk in front of the school. They carried their mariachi instruments. And riding on the back of the leader's bike...

"Benjamin, what in the name of the Lord are you doing?" Wiener screamed.

"*¡Basta ya!*" the man on the front bike screamed. He was easily six and a half feet tall and wielded a length of heavy link chain. "Do not say the name of *el dios muerto* around *El Cazador's Mariachi de Luchador.*"

"Give me back my son!"

"*Aprendiz* is no longer your son. He now belongs to *El Cazador*! He is our new trumpet player!"

"Never!" Wiener yelled, a shitload of single tears

falling from his face.

"It's too late, Dad! I am now *el siervo de Satanás,* and my Lord demands bloodletting," Benjamin yelled.

"En el nombre de Satanás, vamos pesar a los débiles de la tierra," every member of the mariachi band repeated in unison.

Benjamin got off El Cazador's bike. A man near the back walked towards him, holding a large *guitarrón*. He offered the headstock side to Benjamin, who took the neck with both hands and pulled. The neck slid away and the shine of a blade glimmered in the street light.

It was a two-handed, stringed sword.

"Benjamin, think about what you're doing! You've been brainwashed!" Wiener ran towards his son.

El Cazador rose his length of chain and brought it down onto Principal Wiener, striking him hard against the chest. Wiener fell to the ground, a bloody gash now tattooed to his stomach.

"*Cállate, amante de dios*! It is too late now," El Cazador yelled. Benjamin walked towards the school, wielding the sword with poise.

Forrest reached towards him from the ground, but El Cazador whipped his chains once again and slashed his back to ribbons. The pain unbearable, Wiener's consciousness soon slipped away.

"I only know what happened next because the police told me," Wiener told Jane. "Perhaps it's better that way."

Jane noticed Principal Wiener was calming down as he told the story, as if letting out his secrets relieved a burden on his soul. He no longer shook, and his voice had taken on a quiet intensity.

"He swung. He sliced. He thrust. He diced. He turned their insides into rice. My Benjamin killed ten of his classmates before he was carted away," Wiener continued.

"I woke up in the hospital. Police questioned me for days. I told them who was responsible, but according to them, *El Cazador's Mariachi de Luchador* weren't playing the Arts Center that night. It was a different mariachi group. And other than Benjamin's copy of their record, they couldn't find any evidence El Cazador existed.

"Benny was sent to Shady Hills Mental Hospital. My monthly visits brought only pain. He babbled to me about escaping and completing the Dark Lord's mission. After a couple years, I knew all hope was lost. He would never be my sweet little boy again. But now… now, he's back."

The room was silent. Jane looked at him, puzzled.

"Wait, what does all this have to do with the giant, acidic vomit slug in the parking lot?" she asked.

Wiener thought for a moment. "Well… I guess I

don't know."

"*And* there's a serial killer?"

"I'm afraid so, Jane," Wiener said. He circled his desk and walked behind her. "In fact, if you look out that window, you can see him watching us."

Jane approached the window behind Wiener's desk, squinting into the foggy night.

"I can't... see anything," she said, confused, as Wiener grabbed a baseball bat leaning against the far wall.

"I'm sorry, Jane," Wiener muttered.

He swung the wooden bat and cracked Jane across the side of the head. She crumpled to the ground, deadly still on the floor of Wiener's office.

"I'm afraid this is the only way," he said.

He put down the bat, picked Jane up, and set her inside the storage closet next to his desk. He propped her up and shut the door.

"The only way anyone will make it out of this night alive."

Chapter 12

"Pay up, baby!" Sarah spit into Jimbo McKinney's face. "One fat asshole who owes me ten dollars!"

Jimbo was now dressed in short basketball shorts and a stained white wife-beater. He'd lost his van, his suit, and now, the bet.

"Yeah, yeah, bitch," Jimbo mumbled. "As soon as I find my wallet."

"Hey, Jimbo, look on the bright side," Rothschild smiled. "At least you got some action tonight... from Mrs. Poughkeepsie!"

Sarah, Jenny, Jeremy, and Rothschild all guffawed. Poughkeepsie had been telling Officer Briggs to arrest Jimbo for twenty minutes now. He did not want to tell her Sheriff Matthews no longer let him make arrests after one *minor* accident involving a discharged firearm, so he sat, listened, and wiped streams of old-woman spittle from his face.

"Jane really got you good. You've got to hand it to her," Jenny Hibiscus giggled. It seemed to

Jeremy that his love was now having a grand ol' time tonight, their disappointing dinner behind them.

"I'm gonna *kill* that bitch," Jimbo said. "When I find my van, I'm gonna plow her right over with it."

"Okay, apparently, our prick of a synth player decided to up and leave the band, so we're now a four-piece!" Paul Score shouted into the microphone from on-stage before breaking into the timeless guitar line from "Time After Time." Bernard Hook, accepting he had the least important role in the band, now played keys. His bass guitar sat sadly at the back of the stage, unheard, like every other bass in history.

"*Ugh*, this is my favorite song!" Sarah said, taking Rothschild's hand. "What a *great night*!"

She dragged him onto the dance floor. Jeremy and Jenny wrapped around each other, as did every couple in the gym.

"Fuck Crazy Jane. Fuck Mrs. Poughkeepsie," Jimbo muttered. "I'm gonna find some *new* pussy."

By the gym doors, Poughkeepsie fell silent for the first time in almost half an hour, her ears perked.

"This is it, Briggs. The big, popular slow number," Mrs. Poughkeepsie spat. "This is where we'll really get them."

"Barb, ma'am, I really have to get going. Officer

Matthews has to be wondering where I am," Officer Briggs moaned.

"In the name of the Lord, it's a carnival of sin!" Poughkeepsie flapped to the dance floor, eager to bring God back to the gymnasium. Briggs took the opportunity to slip out the gym door, free at last.

It was Leslie's idea to go to the cafetorium.

Alex could barely believe it. Leslie and Alex were behind the giant red curtain of the school's small stage, cuddling on the backstage couch the actors hung out on between scenes.

He was going to lose his virginity. He could feel it. The weight tying him to loserdom would soon be lifted, and he could swim to the surface of having respect for himself.

Plus, he was in love, and they were here, together, at the spot where that love first flourished. He remembered practices for *Arsenic and Old Lace*, where the two would have backstage competitions to see who could blow Alex's prop bugle the loudest without getting yelled at by the director.

They'd had a lot of laughs over the last six months. The bugle, the silly costumes, the Sandy van Thorpe impressions, the silly fantasies of everything from a motorized gym teacher to a puffin-themed muffin shop.

The nostalgia brought a smile onto Alex's face.

"What are *you* smiling about?" Leslie laughed. They were laying down on the puffy couch, arms tangled together, looking deeply into each other's eyes.

"About how you're the best," Alex answered. He tilted his head and leaned in for a kiss, a long embrace, his tongue playfully grazing Leslie's front teeth.

After the incident with Mrs. Poughkeepsie, Leslie suggested they find somewhere more private. She just wanted to be alone with him with no one telling them they couldn't touch and no Cheg Larsons pummeling them into each other.

She knew they wouldn't get this time later. If they tried to watch a movie at her house, her dad would sit down and watch it with them. He'd find reasons to knock on her bedroom door at the most inopportune times, and they'd have to pretend they were only studying. Part of Leslie was even surprised he didn't show up to the prom as a surprise chaperone!

Oh, Dad, she thought. She knew it only came out of love, out of protection. Leslie loved her father. They'd been through so much together. They'd both lost the most important person in their lives.

But he couldn't hold on forever. He had to accept she wouldn't always be his "little pumpkin." Leslie couldn't make him see, though, that he wasn't losing her to the ravages of disease, but to the trials of adulthood.

She forced her dad out of her mind, so she could focus only on Alex. His handsome face, his dark, shaggy head of hair, the way his body felt up against hers.

"Nobody's going to walk in on us, you know," she reminded him, trying to materialize her intentions.

"Are you sure you're ready?" Alex whispered.

"Never been more sure of anything," Leslie answered.

Alex's hands gripped the zipper on the back of Leslie's sky-blue dress and whisked it to her lower back. The dress fell away onto the couch. Leslie slowly unbuttoned her man's dress shirt — he was too busy staring at the lingerie exposed before him.

Alex's chest was flat, lacking in muscle but cute. She saw impressions of his ribs through his body, but she knew hers poked out as well. Alex threw his shirt off and began working on Leslie's bra, twisting and pulling with the intense concentration of one dismantling an atomic bomb.

Thankfully, Leslie's chest was not nuclear-charged, as poor Alex had no chance against the formidable foe.

"Here, let me show you." Leslie set her hands on top of Alex's and guided them in, up, and out. Her bra loosened in Alex's paws, and he lifted the garment off, like a game show contestant eager to see what was behind door number one. The answer: breasts.

"I love you," Alex said, looking back up towards Leslie's face.

"I love you, too," Leslie whispered passionately, as they both slipped off their last pieces of defense.

Leslie closed her eyes and let the feelings wash over her. She hoped this would never end. Alex thought obsessively of dead kittens, naked grandmas, and dead, naked kitten grandmas to try and make sure it wouldn't.

"Oh, Leslie..."

"I love you, Alex..."

"I love you, too..."

"Oh, Alex..."

"Oh, *Leslie*! Uhh... uhhh... *AHHHH!!!!!*"

Leslie had never heard a boy ejaculate before. It sounded more painful than she imagined. Even afterwards, the small groans Alex was letting out didn't sound like he was reeling in ecstasy.

She felt something drip onto her pelvis. First a couple drops and then buckets' worth of liquid.

What in the...

Leslie opened her eyes and let out an ear-shattering scream.

Alex hung suspended in mid-air above her, held up by a three-foot-long machete shoved right between his buttocks. Blood ran from his mouth, a look equal parts pleasure, pain and confusion on his face.

The machete was thrust cleanly through his penis, the wilting organ sliced in two, like cured meat ready for the party platter. The tip of the machete hung at attention, covered in a mixture of bodily fluids.

Leslie screamed, not in sexual delight but visceral fear. Behind her true love, wiggling the machete back and forth and dumping chunks of mangled colon from Alex's backside, was a tall man in a trench coat, a red-and-black mask hugged tight to his face.

This can't be real, she thought. *Wake up, stupid... wake up!*

Alex faded from life, his last vision his mangled manhood, his last sound his lover screaming for help. It all felt unfair, ripped from the most important moment of his life as quickly, as violently as this. He wouldn't live to see that the mythologizing of one's first time was just another farce fed to him, that two minutes of friction was that and nothing more.

Leslie dug her elbows into the couch and tried to back away from the marauder without falling off the side. Screaming, she lashed out with her bare feet, aiming for her attacker. She instead kicked

Alex in the chest, knocking his testicles out of their severed sack and sending one of them rolling towards stage left.

The man gripped his machete with strength and thrust Alex towards her, nine inches of blade protruding from his groin. The blade penetrated Leslie's inner leg, leaving a large, new gash. Leslie's mouth dried out, unable to scream through the pain.

The murderous killer stabbed over and over, catching her in the thigh, the belly, the crotch. Gallons of blood soaked into the old, fluffy couch below her.

She dropped her right hand to cover her wounds and caught a jab. The machete sliced off her pinky and ring fingers and sent them into the crack between couch cushions. Alex lurched back and forth, testicles swinging like a hypnotherapist's pendulum.

Leslie felt woozy from blood loss. She realized what was happening. This could be it. The big shebang. The end of her life.

It couldn't be. This wasn't how it worked. She had a scholarship to Indiana University for the fall. Her dad would drive her to Bloomington in August. And Alex was going there too. They would stay together. They would study theater. They would work their way up to gigs as understudies, eventually take on Broadway, even if it was just as part of the crew.

Her life wasn't supposed to end here, on a dirty couch, naked, bleeding out.

Oh, Mom... if you're watching up there, I need help! I need help now!

The thought of her mother forced her up off the couch. She pushed against Alex's dead body with all the might she could muster. It was just enough. The killer went tumbling backwards, Alex landing on top of him.

Leslie threw herself off the couch and crawled towards the front of the stage. Her first goal: the red velvet curtain, the same deep color as the blood dripping from her body.

The stretch from the couch to the curtain seemed endless. She thought of her first time in front of a crowd, how she could barely bring herself to walk out from backstage and in front of all those eyes.

If I could do that, I can do this.

Two eyes that were always in the crowd were her father's. He never missed a show. He was always there for her, and she wanted to be there for him tomorrow, hugging him and telling him prom had been great. She couldn't imagine his face if he found his daughter's naked corpse onstage. It was the one show she wanted him to miss.

She thought of her dad having to lose the two

things most important to him. She saw the pain, the anger, the all-encompassing death of the soul he went through after losing her mom. She couldn't make him go through that again. She had to live. For Dad.

The curtain was inches away. She pulled and crawled. Then, a groan from behind her. She whipped her head around. The masked man was wiping some entrails off of his trench coat.

He was up. And now he was walking towards her.

Leslie sobbed, crawling as fast as her arms and legs would take her. The pain radiating through her lacerated body meant nothing now, blocked by adrenaline.

Almost... there...

She put her hands on the pulley that controlled the draw curtain. And then felt a long hand grasp each side of her little head.

Leslie screamed as she felt herself lift off the ground. Her temples ached with pressure as the killer took her five feet high, turning her around to stare her right in the face. He shoved the back of her neck against one half of the pulley, then used one hand to string a knot around her neck with the strong rope.

"Please... no..." Leslie sobbed in pity, looking the man in the eyes. She could see no compassion, no humanity in the man. She knew it was hopeless when he smiled a twisted, knowing grin.

"Sorry, my lovely, but it appears… it's curtains for you." He stroked her cheek with the tips of his fingers before gripping the other side of the pulley and tugging it, pulling Leslie higher and higher up the rope.

As she rose towards the ceiling, Leslie thought of her mother, how cruelly and slowly she had been taken away from her and her dad. And as the noose around her neck began to blot out the world around her, she wished for only one thing: to see her one last time.

Everyone talked of their life flashing before their eyes as they crossed into the hereafter. She could once again see Mom, doting, youthful, reading her bedtime stories and tucking her in super tight to protect against the things that went bump in the night.

Or she could receive a vision of Mom, up there, waiting for her. Calling her up to the skies, where they would be reunited once more. Where she could be held. Where she could feel Mom's spindly fingers run through her tufts of hair.

But as the pressure of the rope crushed her windpipe and the life inside her eyes faded away, Leslie Deakins saw absolutely nothing.

Chapter 13

"Jeremy! *Jeremy!*"

He was drowning. The ice-cold water splashed across his face, and he jolted awake, sucking in a deep breath of oxygen to keep himself alive.

No. He was in the gym, not the ocean. He was sitting at one of the tables by the snack layout, facing the dancefloor. Jenny stood to his left, taking his pulse. Rothschild, Sarah, and Jimbo framed her. To his right was Coach Kumin, who held an empty water cup in his hands.

Jenny crouched to his level and touched his shoulder. "Jeremy… you passed out again."

And then he remembered everything.

Approaching Leslie Deakins and Alex Spence.

Disemboweling the poor kid.

Stringing Leslie up by the curtain.

But, no… it wasn't him who did it. It was…

Oh my god, he thought. *The killer's at the prom.*

Jeremy bolted up, but wooziness overcame him.

He sat back down in the chair and looked up at Jenny, who was on the verge of tears. Coach Kumin, his job done, went back to the snacks.

"Jeremy, sit down. Something's wrong. You need to rest," Jenny said.

"Something horrible's happened," Jeremy said quietly, staring out at his blissfully unaware classmates dancing in front of him.

"Jeremy, what are you talking about?" Jenny asked.

"Maybe he hit his head..." Rothschild whispered to Sarah.

"Yesterday, when I passed out in Hamburger Heaven... I saw something," Jeremy said, more commanding this time. "A massacre. At a mental hospital. And then I woke up... and Officer Briggs was yelling about murders at Shady Hills."

"Wait..."

"And then, after you dropped me off, Jenny, I passed out again," he continued. "I saw Douglas Whitehead killed... in real time. And now he's nowhere to be seen."

"Buddy, Douglas Whitehead is the last person I'd expect to see at the prom," Rothschild said. "That doesn't mean he's dead."

Jeremy looked into Rothschild's eyes, a shell-shocked stupor in his eyes. "Are Leslie Deakins and Alex Spence here?"

"Yeah, I saw them, like, half an hour ago," Rothschild said.

"No, are they here *now*?"

The group glanced around the dance floor. "I don't see them," Sarah answered.

"That's because they're dead."

Everyone fell silent, except for The Gentlemen, whose take on Bananarama's "Venus" did not fit the vibe.

Jimbo broke the silence. "What the fuck are you talking about?"

"Leslie and Alex are dead. I watched them get killed."

"Jeremy, baby, I've been with you all night. What do you mean, you *watched* them get killed?" Jenny said.

"I told you, I'm… seeing things. I don't know why. Or how. But I am," Jeremy stammered. He was treading on shaky ground. One false move and his telepathic secret was history.

"Somebody get Shady Hills on the phone… I think we've got a new patient here," Jimbo said. Jenny got up and slapped him across the face.

"What is *wrong* with you? We need to get him help, not make fun of him," Jenny yelled at Jimbo.

"Jenny, I don't need any help. There's nothing wrong with me… there's something wrong *here*. In this school. Tonight. Somebody is here, and we need to get out... now," Jeremy said, louder than before.

Jenny crouched to Jeremy's side and put her pointer finger to his mouth. "*Shh...* Jeremy, somebody's going to hear you."

Jeremy felt like screaming. His best friends in the whole world all thought he had gone nuts.

An image of his Uncle Mark flashed in his mind. *Stay strong, Jeremy.*

"Now, buddy, know that none of us here think you're crazy," Rothschild said, putting a hand on Jeremy's shoulder. "It's just that you're acting really crazy."

Jeremy brushed his hand off. "Well, then, let's go look. If Leslie and Alex aren't dead in the cafetorium, go ahead and lock me up in the loony bin."

"But wait," Jimbo said. "What if Leslie and Alex are just dead in the auditorium from boning too hard? Or slipping on a wet floor? How will we know they got murdered?"

Jeremy stared into Jimbo's eyes. "Trust me, you'll know."

Jimbo turned to Rothschild and circled his finger around his ear. "*Cuckoo.*"

Jenny stood up and pushed him away. "You're gonna stay here, asshole. The rest of us will go," she said.

"Fine with me," Jimbo said. "I'm gonna find some bitches."

He disappeared into the dance floor, as the rest of the gang left the gym to make the long walk across the school to the cafetorium.

Jenny grabbed Jeremy's hand and squeezed as they walked, hugging on to his left shoulder. Even if he was going crazy, she still loved him. What would they find in the auditorium? Nothing at all? A couple making love? Or something much worse?

Rothschild thought fear was a waste of time. Even if there was a murderer loose in Barbara Falls, he figured he would come out the other side unscathed. Humans are cocky that way.

Sarah Farrow wished they were back in the gym. She only got one senior prom in her life, and she was currently missing her favorite song. Besides, it was a quarter to ten, and if this took too long, she would miss the royalty ceremony. This was *totally* uncool.

They arrived at the auditorium doors. Jeremy walked ahead and stood in front. Jenny's heart raced. She nodded to him, signaling she was ready.

He opened the door.

The cafetorium was silent. The lunch tables were folded up and set along the back of the cafeteria area, leaving a wide, empty space leading to the stage. The red velvet curtain on stage was slightly ajar, but nothing else was out of the ordinary.

"See, dude. Nothing wrong," Rothschild whispered, unsure why he was talking so quietly. Sarah sighed in relief and looked at her watch.

"Not here... backstage," Jeremy said and walked towards the curtain. The others followed.

The sound of heels and dress shoes on linoleum flooring reverberated through the empty room.

Click. Clack.

Clomp. Clomp.

Jeremy tip-toed up the staircase on the side of the stage and walked through the curtain. Jenny's heart eased towards her throat. Even the iron-willed Rothschild began to shake.

The stage was dark, two dim safety lights casting long, askew shadows against the sets of black curtains across the stage.

"I can't... see anything," Jenny whispered. In the gymnasium, none of this felt real, but back here, anything felt possible.

"I think there's a light by the pulley," Jeremy said.

"I got it," Rothschild said. He took slow steps towards the pulley. As he took his last steps, he felt something cold and hard brush against his face. He swept it away. *Just the rope pulley,* he thought.

His hand found the light switch, and a series of overhead lights flickered on.

Sarah screamed. Rothschild looked up.

Hanging from the pulley was Leslie Deakins, more naked than the day she was born. Her face was a deep blue, her eyes bulged to the extent of their sockets. She had been stabbed brutally in the stomach, and her genitals looked more like roadkill. One of her legs had been sawed… or maybe chewed… down to the bone, stray scraps of flesh the only cover for her tibia. Her skin was pale and veiny, her limbs rigid and still.

Jeremy clasped his eyes shut. His dreams were now confirmed as reality.

Sarah dropped to her knees, ripping her throat to pieces with pained cries. Rothschild, now realizing Leslie's bony toes were what tickled his face, tensed every muscle in his body before yelping in incredulity and running back towards his girlfriend.

Jenny Hibiscus backed away from the body. The violent shaking of her legs made walking in heels a momentous struggle.

"Jesus, Jeremy! Jesus *fucking* Christ!" Rothschild yelled. "What the hell did you drag us into?"

"No… no… no…" Sarah repeated.

Rothschild grabbed her hand and ran into the cafeteria. "C'mon, we're getting out of here. Now!"

The words sparked another vision in Jeremy's mind. Vague, effervescent, more a feeling than a daydream.

A feeling that if they walked out that door, it would be the last time he saw them alive.

"No, guys! Wait!" Jeremy ran after them. Jenny stood backstage, comatose, waiting for someone to wake her from this awful nightmare.

Sarah Farrow's mind was now far away from dreams of being prom queen; in fact, her mind was far away from nearly everything. She was vaguely aware Rothschild was pulling her towards the back door of the school, but everything around her was a blur. Her mind had retreated back to her youth, the vibrant red blood backstage replaced by the comforting red tiles of Connect Four games and tricycles.

Rothschild was determined to get out of this alive and bring his girl with him. Dragging Sarah by one hand behind him, he kicked open the back door and rushed through the back parking lot. His beast of a pickup truck was parked out front, and they needed to circle the whole school to get to it.

Jeremy followed closely behind. Images of a car crash were flashing inside his head, becoming more and more vivid as he ran. He had to stop it; he barely even realized he had left poor Jenny all by her lonesome inside.

"Rothschild, wait! Please!" he yelled to no avail.

Inside the cafetorium, Jenny broke out of her miniature coma. She looked again at the mangled body of Leslie Deakins and started to dry heave.

Even if Alex Spence was more alive than his girlfriend, she wasn't going to stick around to find him. She ran from the scene as fast as her heeled feet would take her, determined never to set foot in the Barbara Falls High cafetorium ever again.

Rothschild was first to the truck. He slammed the hood like the winner of a race and rifled through his pockets for the keys.

"Please, Rothschild, no! Let's go inside and plan our next move! We're safer together!" Jeremy yelled out as he approached the car.

"Get in the truck then! We're fucking out of here, man!" Rothschild said.

Jeremy decided saving his friends' lives was more important than keeping his secret.

"Rothschild, listen to me. If you get into that car with Sarah, it'll be the last time you do. I don't know how I know, but I know," he said.

Rothschild looked at him incredulously. "What the hell is this, Jeremy? First, you're seeing visions... now you're seeing the future? Fuck you, man. Sarah, get in the car."

Rothschild opened the driver's side door to the pickup, but before he could get in, Jeremy ran to it and slammed it shut. Rothschild pushed him away from the car. Sarah stood behind him, helpless.

"Jeremy, I don't want to hurt you, but I *will*, man,"

Rothschild said. They both stood in front of the pickup door, arms out, ready for the other to make the next move.

Then, they heard Jenny scream.

Jeremy jerked his head back. Jenny was standing by the front door of the school. He expected to see the killer approaching her, lusting for death. Instead, she was all alone by the door, screaming and staring down Main Street.

Thank God she's safe, Jeremy thought. *But what is she screaming about?*

Rothschild caught on a little quicker. He whipped his head towards Main Street just in time to see Pat van Martens' Ford Falcon hurtling towards them, Pat's foot having chosen the car's gas pedal as its final resting place.

The car's bloody windshield signaled their fate. They had no chance.

The Falcon smashed into Rothschild's pickup truck at eighty miles an hour. Sarah and Rothschild's bodies became one for the last time, thousands of pounds of metal crushing their bones together and romantically exchanging splinters of rib and femur.

Jeremy, farther to the side of the car, only had half of the bones in his body shattered to dust. He looked out at Jenny from the pavement. He realized he couldn't feel anything below his waist. And above his waist was only crippling pain. He reached out to his love, watching her fall to the ground and douse the sidewalk below in tears.

Jeremy Vernon thought to himself how lame it was that his psychic powers could tell him what song The Gentlemen were going to play next, but couldn't tell him he was about to get hit by a car.

Then, the gas line of Rothschild's truck caught fire, and Jeremy Vernon thought no more.

Chapter 14

The forest surrounding Barbara Falls is dense and suffocating. In the daytime, legions of bushy fir trees blot out the sun. At night, the tree cover makes the darkness feel even darker.

The area does not see many campers or hikers for a reason. Walking around, you know there is something *wrong* with these woods. It could be the unending stillness. Or the twisted shadows the towering trees cast on the forest floor. Or something more malevolent, something unseen, something felt in the back of your throat like a pesky cough.

Mark Vernon drove through this strange wilderness, the malevolence surrounding him on all sides. The roads were deserted; he hadn't flipped off his brights in the last twenty miles. They still were not strong enough, though, to penetrate the darkness threatening to swallow him.

Before now, he'd never made the 14-hour trip from Salt Lake City. He knew he wasn't welcome.

His brother, Brian, hadn't even sent him his new address.

Mark knew he scared "Dr. Brian," as their dad had called him even before he started his own practice. His brother was always logical, left-brained, lacking in imagination. Mark's head had been in the clouds since he came out of the womb.

He was even the reason Brian moved his family to this nowheresville of a town. The doctor had to make sure Jeremy could live a normal life, and the psychic connection his son shared with Mark was too bizarre, too unbelievable, too silly.

Now, Uncle Mark had a feeling their psychic connection was Jeremy's only chance to make it through this night alive.

His brother always believed Mark's faith in such hocus-pocus was because of his copious drug use. The truth was deeper. Mark used substances not to escape normal life, but to try and understand a semblance of it.

Mark grew up just like Jeremy, with the ability to hear inside people's heads. Throughout his life, Mark tried to strip himself from this horrible curse any way he could: hard drugs, loud music, fast women. By 30, his powers had dissipated almost entirely. Now, at 45, there was nothing left.

Until yesterday. A white, searing pain had echoed through his temples at work, a migraine that keeled him over in shock.

What he saw when he winced his eyes shut was even worse. Teenagers brutally murdered on dirt roads. A mental hospital caked in blood. And his poor nephew in the middle of all of it. Once the headache lessened, he went home sick and was on his way, determined to see Jeremy for the first time in almost ten years.

A life spent wading in mediocrity and normalcy had taught Mark he never should have let his powers slip away. And when Jeremy was younger, he tried to impart that lesson, helping him hone his powers into a gift rather than a curse.

Only a few are born special. Even fewer do anything with the talents they're given. Mark had tried to make his nephew an exception.

Now, Jeremy was in danger. And Uncle Mark knew, if he failed him again, it would be the last time he ever would.

Mark passed a sign. "8 Miles to Barbara Falls." He put more weight onto the gas pedal. Eight more miles in this forest still seemed like a lifetime.

He felt eyes staring at him from inside the trees. Animals? Or perhaps the judging eyes of his brother, chastising him for being a burnout, a nobody, a wacko?

Tonight would be his chance to tell those eyes how wrong they were.

Jenny couldn't move.

Her lip quivered against her will, but the rest of her body was stone-still. She stared at the blaze, wanting to go help Jeremy, hold him in her arms one last time. Instead, she stood, mouth agape, eyes bulged, her pyre of friends suffocating her mind.

Officer Robert Briggs had watched the incident occur from the police cruiser. Briggs, not noticing the rotting lump of sheriff by the school's front door, had been waiting for Matthews in the safety of the vehicle. Disaster, however, had come to him.

He ran to the scene, over to Jenny. He grabbed her and joggled her by the shoulders.

"Jenny! Jenny, are you okay?" Briggs yelled in her ear. The glaze surrounding Jenny's eyes fell away, and she stared into Briggs' terrified pupils.

"Jeremy… is Jeremy going to be okay?" she asked with childlike expectancy.

"No… Jeremy's dead. You saw the crash, right? Nobody could live through that," Briggs said.

Jenny broke her stare and collapsed into tears on Briggs' shoulder. Briggs wrapped his arms tightly around her, wondering where Matthews was. Without the sheriff, it was *his* job to do actual police work. He shuddered at the thought.

"Jenny. Jenny, honey, I need you to go back to the gym. I'm going to call the Seneca fire department. You have to stay calm, even though your life is now in shambles. Be strong, Jenny."

Briggs ran towards the front office, pulling out his taser, the only firearm the sheriff allowed him to carry. Having anything in his hands made him feel just a bit safer.

The school's lobby was empty. Ticket collectors Rachel and Corey were in the gymnasium, waiting for the climactic crowning under ten minutes away.

Outside, Jenny stared at the wreck, her eyes drawn to the blaze like a moth.

She didn't notice the pair of globular creatures, one now the size of a grizzly bear, slowly crawling towards her from the back parking lot.

Inside, Briggs kicked in the office door, even though it was unlocked. He grabbed the phone on Nancy's desk, holding the phone in one hand and pushing 9-1-1 on the keypad with the tip of the taser.

He held the phone to his ear. Nothing. Not even a dial tone.

He'd have to put out the blaze himself. He looked around and saw a gleaming red fire extinguisher on the far wall.

He grabbed the extinguisher with his free hand, still waving the taser in the air, just in case another speeding car came through the ceiling. He ran back outside to the fiery wreck.

"I told you to go inside, Jenny! For God's sake,

stop being such a child!" Briggs lifted the extinguisher and sprayed the conflagration of metal and skin. Waving the tool like a madman, he successfully blotted out most of the fire.

He turned back towards Jenny, ready to let loose another spray, this time of encouraging words. But then he saw the horrifying monsters slithering towards them.

Briggs let out a feminine scream and tightened his grip on the extinguisher, sending a stream of foam rocketing into his face. The shock of impact loosened his trigger finger, and he shot the darts of his taser gun right into his neck.

He fell backwards and screamed bloody murder, which only sent more toxic chemicals down his throat. He was utterly blind. His arms swung around wildly until he came into contact with something large and squishy.

Jenny? He thought hopefully.

It was not Jenny.

The creature devoured him whole, vomit spittle melting right through the layer of extinguisher foam covering his face. As his flesh dissolved in an orgiastic sensation of pain, Briggs still felt rather content about the best day of police work he had ever had.

Jenny, her mind scrambled by fear and confusion, let out a whimper and ran towards the wreck, hoping Jeremy could help her escape this nightmare. She wrapped her arms around her lover, clasping shut her eyes and letting Jeremy's comforting warmth transport her to better times.

Jeremy didn't have much warmth to give, as Jeremy was a skeleton. His blackened rib-cage, still clothed in a few barbecued strands of mangled flesh, crumbled in Jenny's arms, sending ash down her dress and into her bosom.

She opened her eyes and Jeremy's skinless skull fell into her outstretched arms.

Then and there, Jenny Hibiscus' bright blue pupils lost their glean, her lovely, childlike innocence decomposing alongside her boyfriend's body. She stared into the nonexistent eyeballs of the skull in her palms and screamed the loudest scream she had ever let out.

She threw the skull like a hot potato. It flew towards the creatures, landing on top of the smaller one. Its vaginal mouth opened wide to greet the remains hurtling towards it, but when bone met gelatin, the slug let out a high-pitched dog-whistle of a squeak. The thing's jelly flesh sizzled and popped like bacon grease as it screeched relentlessly.

Soon, the smaller creature was only a dissolved puddle on the sidewalk. Its larger brethren showed no care for its broodmate, still shambling towards the human female before it.

The atrocity exhibition in front of her restored Jenny's faded mind and awoke her from her catatonia.

It loves to eat human flesh when it's alive, Jenny thought. *But when it's dead, it kills them.*

Jenny looked at her crisped boyfriend and realized Jeremy had made a sacrifice for her from beyond the grave. She picked up his cremated torso and chucked it at the approaching blob. As the monster screeched in pain, she sprinted towards the school.

Once safe inside, she slammed shut the double doors and looked around. The muffled sounds of music and conversations reverberated into the foyer, but the rest of the school was silent.

Portions of blistered, rank skin melted from the creature's body outside, but the dead boy's dust wasn't enough to do it in completely. The nauseous creature from Hell squirmed along its trail of slime towards the school.

Inside, Jenny pushed over the table in front of the gym doors, and slid it against the entrance. She ran to the front office, desperate for reinforcements. She shuffled Nancy's crossword puzzles to the ground as she rummaged through every inch of the reception desk. She opened up the bottom drawer and found a stack of 2x4s, a bucket of nails, and a hammer.

"I guess these'll just have to do," she sighed.

Jenny ferociously nailed the front doors shut, a buoyant bravery coursing through her. She had adhered three boards to each side before the creature reached her. She'd lost her cool for a second, but now, she was back to her resourceful self.

Unbeknownst to him, Jenny *had* kept a secret or two from Jeremy in their relationship. Hidden, tucked away, nearly forgotten little secrets, those of her grandfather. Granpappy Hibiscus, a stone-faced immigrant from the Austro-Hungarian empire, had been somewhere between a survivalist and a sociopath. When she was young, he had taught her, his favorite granddaughter, survival tips: how to shoot a gun, start a fire, hide in a bucket for immigration purposes, skin a deer, kill a Soviet, skin a Soviet and hide inside it for warmth.

As she watched the creature approach, open its mouth-like socket and spray the front doors with chunky, yellow-green bile, she thanked Granpappy in her mind. The man, who by all other accounts was a terrible father and grandfather, had died four years prior. She wondered what strange Hungarian babbling he was cursing at her up from Heaven.

The monster vomit could melt through skin, but not through glass. She was safe. For now.

She nailed one more board to each side. Behind her, Principal Wiener slipped out of the office for the first time that night, a large, bulging backpack strapped to his back. He did not say a word to Jenny nor remark on the giant gonorrheal slug vomiting on the front doors of his high school.

The creature gave up and slid back into the night. From inside the gym, Jenny could hear the muffled start of the crowning ceremony, right on time.

"Thank you all for coming to the 1987 Barbara Falls High Senior Prom," she heard Sandy van Thorpe announce.

She took a deep breath. Two of the nominees were dead. Homicidal vagina-worms roamed the streets. Leslie Deakins' naked body was strung up and gnawed to bits in the cafeteria. And, here, everyone she knew was giving their full attention to a popularity contest.

She had a churning feeling Barbara Falls High's suffering was just beginning.

Chapter 15

"Alright, all, it is 9:45! In fifteen minutes, you will know your 1987 Barbara Falls High Prom King and Queen!" Deborah Moyet announced from the stage. Applause came mostly from Brittany Beverly and her troupe of loyal followers.

"Before we leave the stage for the crowning ceremony, here's one of my personal favorites... this one's called 'Perfect Way.'"

Bernard Hook filled in on synth badly, while Steven Sylvian struggled to keep up with the drum part after three flasks of Evan Williams.

Meanwhile, Brittany Beverly practiced her victory speech again and again in her head, making sure she had every word perfect. Her brain was not the most capable in the gymnasium, and this was the hardest she'd ever made it work.

She had written a speech guaranteed to leave no dry eyes in the house. One month ago, she had visited the local library for the first time, borrowed the VHS single of "We Are the World," and pulled out all the important parts. Soon, the whole school would know she was beautiful *and* caring.

"Right this very moment, there are kids in Africa dying of starvation," her moving speech began. "Luckily, I am not one of them, so I can be your Prom Queen."

On the other side of the dance floor, Mr. Stannaker suffered through a dance with one of his least favorite students, Kimberly "Piggy" Donner. The first problem with Kimberly: she was fat. The second problem: she still talked to him despite being fat, not understanding he'd rather be talking to someone less fat.

"Thanks for dancing with me, Mr. Stannaker," Kimberly said to him, a wide smile on her face. "Nobody else would."

"Yeah, yeah, Kimberly," Stannaker said. "Enjoy it while it lasts."

Stannaker had his eyes set on the bodacious blonde junior attached to Brad Fahey's arm, whose name escaped him at the moment. He would dance with her tonight, dip her grades next week, and then have her in for an after-school session of "tutoring." Worked every time.

From the back of the gymnasium, Rachel Severinsen chuckled. Next to her, Corey carried the paper Hamburger Heaven bag in his hand, anxious to unleash the best prank Barbara Falls had ever seen.

"She's gonna *flip*," Corey said.

"She'll lose her loser mind," Rachel agreed. They stared down their enemy, who stood off-stage, waiting for her moment.

The only one in the gym not ready for The Gentlemen to stop playing was Dick Wong-Dick, who would've given himself a hernia if he boogied any more violently to the music.

Wong-Dick, not well-versed in American pop music, believed every tune the band had played throughout the show was an original song, and he was now convinced this was the best band in the United States. Even better, though, was Deborah Moyet, who had somehow gotten even more beautiful since Wong-Dick had spoken to her. He caught her staring and smiling right at him throughout the set, and his heart backflipped each time.

Cheg Larson had grown tired of moshing, and now had moved on to spitting on things. He spit in the punch bowl, he spit in Piggy Donner's hair, he spit at the band onstage. He even spit on himself, which got him so pissed, he almost punched himself in the face.

Despite his mischief making, he thought it was about time to leave prom and have a more metal time elsewhere with Pat. He decided to stay only for the crowning ceremony, so he could boo whoever won Prom Queen. That would show 'em.

Jimbo McKinney was wondering why his friends were taking so damn long, even if there *was* a dead body in the cafetorium. He was all alone and was now bored. The only thing left for him to do was find a new woman to prey on.

He set his eyes on a plain-looking girl sitting alone at one of the tables by the snack bar. Jimbo thought he had a class with the girl, but her face was too nondescript for him to know for sure.

The girl's name was Abigail Williams, and she was first-chair trumpet player of the Barbara Falls High Jazz Band. If anyone knew Abigail was plain-looking, it was Abigail herself. It was her main preoccupation. Despite her triumphant trumpeting talent, marvelous mathematical mind, and heart-wrenchingly heartfelt heart, Abigail had been so thoroughly ignored by the opposite sex throughout her life that she now had the self-confidence of a ground squirrel. This meekness amplified her plainness, and the vicious cycle continued.

She was just Jimbo's type: breathing. He smiled at her from the dance floor. Abigail smiled back, if only at the memory of his naked mile an hour earlier. Taking this as an invitation, Jimbo went in for the kill.

"This is a perfect way to make the girls go crazy…" Deborah Moyet sang, and the band began to wrap up the Scritti Politti classic.

Their second set had sounded horrible. Moyet couldn't believe McCluskey would leave during their biggest gig yet. Luckily, their ticket to Japanese stardom was still in the crowd, swinging his limbs around without even a concept of rhythm.

"Alright, boys and girls, we'll be back for the prom royalty's first dance! Don't go anywhere!" Moyet yelled into the mic to polite applause. She turned towards the band and told them she'd stay inside this break. They were not heartbroken.

As the boys headed off stage, Moyet turned back towards the crowd and nearly tackled Sandy van Thorpe, who now stood center stage. Sandy flashed her a smug grin and outreached her hand for the mic.

Deborah handed it to her, put on the smile that always got her what she wanted, and walked straight for Dick Wong-Dick. Dick could hardly believe it. Maybe this *was* the land of opportunity after all.

The rest of the band walked through the foyer and continued to the back entrance. No one stopped them along the way. The members of the band without heaving breasts were used to getting fewer compliments, but this was worse than usual.

"That was absolute *shit,*" Paul Score said to himself. "I'm going to beat that twat McCluskey to the fucking ground when I see him."

Bernard Hook moped silently. Steven Sylvian, too drunk to form a coherent response, snorted and hiccupped.

They exited into the back parking lot. A thick layer of fog now surrounded the lot, as if a cloud had smoked some reefer and forgotten where the sky was.

"Jesus, I can hardly see out here," Score said.

He squinted his way to the van, lit up a cigarette, and attempted to puff away mediocrity. The other two did the same. Score continued to complain, but then he realized he wasn't the only one talking in the parking lot.

Someone, somewhere very close by, was muttering in a foreign language. Score's white ears couldn't tell, but perhaps… Spanish?

As they approached the van, the muttering got louder. Score, cigarette hanging in his hand, listened closer and leaned his head against the van. His eyes widened.

"Someone's in the van," he said.

"Some Mexican is trying to steal our gear!" Hook yelled. He dropped his cigarette to the ground, pushed past Score, and swung open the back doors of the van.

An ocean of blood spilled out onto Hook's suede shoes. He was too busy gawping in horror to notice. A pentagram drawn in nature's red paint adorned the roof of the van. Below, black candles circled the sigil. In the middle of the circle was a masked man, sitting cross-legged, a skull of a goat clutched in his hands. In a foreign tongue, he continued to babble despite the intrusion on his unholy rites.

"*Y Satanás, mi padre y mi guía, poseen estos paganos con su magia. Haz que tus esclavos... y los míos,*" the man uttered.

"What the fuck are you doing in our van?" Hook screamed.

The man looked up. His smile, visible through his red and black mask, looked sinister in the dim light of the black candles.

"Oh, will you look at that? Just the *gentlemen* I wanted to see," he said.

The goat's skull in his hands began to glow bright red.

Hook had time to blurt out one final expletive before a pair of neon rouge lasers shot from the goat's eye cavities into his own eyeballs, locking them open like clamps. A second set of lasers blasted from the skull and gained dominion over Paul Score's peepers.

Sylvian, the furthest from the van, felt the world rush back to him. An avid drunk driver, Sylvian had tried every method, from black coffee to white powder, to sober up before a long drive. He learned then and there the only foolproof way: all-encompassing fear for your life.

He didn't get a chance to test the theory. Sylvian turned to run, but felt two white-hot beams of light burst through the back of his head, filtering his vision neon-red. The parking lot glowed with the vivid rouge of 3D glasses. He shook, shit-scared, for five seconds. Then, his brain started disintegrating.

The three Gentlemen, now without control of their own bodies, opened their mouths wide. Their gullets glowed orange like human jack-o'-lanterns. In a flurry of coughing and gagging, all three choked up chunks of pink brain foam from their mouths. Membrane fell to the ground with satisfying splats.

Soon, their last bits of brain matter, still attached to their spinal cords, dangled from their mouths like spittle. They all stood, motionless, staring at the masked man in the van.

"You are now slaves of Lord Satan and children of El Cazador. You will submit to our every whim," the man said. The bandmates grunted in agreement.

"And what El Cazador requires from you mindless vermin at this time… is to play a little bit of music," he continued.

More grunting ensued.

"But I'm afraid your normal set is over. Your next song will instead be the incantation to awaken Our Lord."

Chapter 16

"Thank you all for coming to the 1987 Barbara Falls High Senior Prom," Sandy van Thorpe announced from the front of the stage.

Sandy never got much attention from her peers. She was a tall, toothy redhead, freckles scattered across her long face. She wasn't unattractive, but Barbara Falls boys avoided her like yellow fever.

The main reason for this was her overbearing, enraging personality, but her wardrobe didn't help. The autumnal-patterned dress she wore this evening looked sewn together out of a quilt and hung loosely enough to cover every trace of her femininity.

Now, none of that mattered. Most of the crowd stared at Sandy in rapt silence, eager to find out who they had voted winner of their own popularity contest.

"I hope everyone has had a magical, unforgettable night so far. There's still an hour left of the dance, but it's now time to crown the Class of 1987 Prom

Royalty."

The crowd went wild. Sandy couldn't hold back a smile at the attention.

"First up: the nominees for Prom King.... Sam Berry!" Applause. Cheers. Sam, six glasses of prom punch deep, only kept his center of balance by clutching his date's ass cheeks for dear life.

"Matt Brady!" Matt let loose a politician's wave to the gymnasium.

"Chris Rothschild!" Eyes searched the gym in vain. Where was Rothschild? Grumbles broke out amongst the crowd.

"Where's your friend, Jimbo?" Abigail asked. She gripped Jimbo's hand with desperation and crushing loneliness.

"Oh, don't worry, Amber. He and Sarah probably went to screw in the bathroom and forgot all about the ceremony," Jimbo laughed.

"Abigail... my name's Abigail."

"Yeah, that's what I said, babe."

"And now, the nominees for Prom Queen. Brittany Beverly!" Brittany showered kisses towards her adoring classmates.

"Sarah Farrow!" The grumbling intensified. There's no way Sarah would miss the crowning ceremony... right?

"And Sandy van Thorpe!" The conversations fell to a hush, and Sandy's name was met with nearly visible silence. Her wide smile dimmed a notch.

The crowd stayed silent as Sandy handed herself an envelope. The tension was unbearable for exactly four members of the audience.

Her spindly fingers ripped open the envelope. As she slowly pulled out a white note card, the only sound in the gymnasium was the smack of her lips as she opened her mouth.

"Our Prom King and Queen are… Matt Brady and Brittany Beverly!"

The crowd hurrahed, Cheg Larson's adamant booing lost amongst the din. Matt embraced Sam and Brad in a very heterosexual bro hug, as Brittany Beverly's beautiful, blonde buddies blubbered in bliss. Matt and Brittany took hold of each other's hands and walked through the sea of adoring faces to the stage.

Jenny Hibiscus burst through the gym doors. The celebratory scene before her was at odds with the horrors outside. Perhaps it wasn't the best time to announce Matt and Brittany's competition were crucified on a scrap-metal cross in the parking lot.

She spied Principal Wiener standing in the far corner of the gym. The intense look in his blood-shot eyes did not assuage her fear one bit.

Brittany and Matt walked onstage and the applause doubled in volume. Tears ran down Brittany's face. This was the only thing that she had ever dreamed of. Matt's minty-fresh smile was on full display. He was ecstatic everyone else *also* believed he was the coolest dude in the town of Barbara Falls.

As the applause died down, Brittany outreached her hand towards Sandy's mic. Every brain cell not spent maintaining her balance in high-heels repeated the words of her speech inside her head.

To her horror, Sandy van Thorpe kept talking.

"Before Mr. Brady and Miss Beverly share their first dance together as prom royalty, I'd like to say a few words as your Class President, head of the prom committee, and soon-to-be valedictorian," Sandy said.

Brittany's jaw dropped. Sandy van *Dork* was ruining everything! Her genius speech spilled from her mind, replaced by pure hatred. She hoped Sandy van *Bitch* would die a horrible death at that very moment. Her face reddened to a shade of rouge deep enough to be seen through her four kilos of makeup.

"Merriam-Webster defines 'school' as an organization that provides instruction," Sandy continued. "But this instruction doesn't just take place in class. It takes place in events like this one: our senior prom."

Matt's smile drained from his face. If Sandy kept going, his glorious after-prom sex session would instead be hours spent listening to Brittany complain. He suddenly felt like throwing up.

"This event, at which I hope you're getting all sorts of life instruction, could not have happened without the Prom Committee, which, of course, is headed by me."

"It's time," Rachel Severinsen, teeth clenched, said to Corey. "Get the bitch."

Corey folded open the crumpled Hamburger Heaven bag. The prank of the decade was about to unfold. He reached his hand in and pulled out the tool to ruin Sandy van Thorpe's night and hopefully the rest of her life.

Corey pulled out a water gun.

"It wasn't easy to single-handedly create a night you'll all remember forever, but I think I did an admirable job," Sandy blabbed. A film began to fall over the eyes of the senior class.

Corey rushed towards the stage, miniature orange squirt gun clutched tight in his hands. Sandy, wrapped up in hearing herself talk, saw nothing coming until she felt a sharp blast of water spray her right in the face.

Corey pumped and sprayed, sending all six ounces of water in the child's plaything towards Sandy. He was sure to ruin her hairdo *and* spray her in the crotch to make it look like she peed herself. It wasn't his first rodeo.

As the last drops ran down Sandy's face, she opened her eyes. She looked out at her classmates. The ones she despised. The ones she tolerated. The teachers she looked up to so much.

Each and every one of them began to laugh. Howls, chuckles, snorts, and honks reverberated through the gymnasium like the echoes of lost love through the annals of time. It was the loudest noise Sandy van Thorpe had ever heard. As she watched Mr. Stannaker bend over in laughter and Jimbo McKinney spit red punch onto Abigail Williams' dress, warm tears started to flow down her freckled face.

Brittany Beverly laughed the hardest of all. *Grody* van Thorpe had ruined *her* special moment and received immediate payback. For a second, she thought maybe she had ESP, as she didn't know the definition of the word and didn't realize ESP did not cause water gun pranks.

As Dick Wong-Dick and Deborah Moyet laughed at the loser, Dick felt a womanly hand run down his spine. His body tensed up. He looked at Deborah.

She was laughing and smiling. And not just at Sandy, but at *him*. An American girl was touching him and looking into his eyes. It was the greatest moment of his life.

On the stage, Matt Brady began to feel a rumbling beneath his feet, as if he were getting a nice foot massage from a cheerleader after a long football practice.

But the season is over, Matt thought. *So what could it be?*

He heard a sound, too. A crunching, a chomping beneath him. But the laughter was too loud. He couldn't put his finger on it.

The laughing wouldn't stop. Sandy, in love with feeling in control, felt her life's work crumble in her spidery hands. She thought nothing could ever stop her from crying.

She was wrong.

One of the floorboards of the plywood stage snapped in two under her left foot. Her foot fell into the hole and she collapsed, falling off balance and snapping her ankle in two places.

She screamed out in pain. The laughter quieted enough to hear the cause of the cave-in.

A dog, viciously snarling beneath her.

Two seconds later, gallons of blood erupted from the stage hole, rocketing up like Old Faithful and showering Brittany and Matt, staining Miss Beverly's yellow dress forever red.

The crowd watched in horror as Sandy's ugly dress was drenched in gore. Her leg twisted deeper and deeper beneath the stage. Splinters of wood gouged holes in her skin, awakening her to vomit-inducing pain.

Sandy screamed as her leg was eviscerated down to nothing and waves of her blood swashed across her teary eyes. She would trade everything, all her achievements, all her test scores, for this pain to end.

When her entire leg had been devoured, the dog from Hell kept on eating, pulling her entire torso through the small, splintering hole. Sandy watched a wood shaving half a foot long penetrate her chest and pierce her large intestine. Half-digested pretzel chunks spewed from the wound.

She could do nothing to stop it. The leg she still had was now bent completely perpendicular to her body. The horrifying display of gymnastics stretched and snapped tendons in her thigh. Still, the dog ate, and she was pulled into the hole like beef into a meat grinder.

Soon, all that was left of Sandy van Thorpe was her blood, splattered on everything from Brittany Beverly's corsage to Coach Kumin's plate of pretzels.

The entire gym was silent. Even Corey Jones, who had collapsed onto the stage floor with Sandy's blood clogging his throat, dared not cough and disturb the silence.

Through the gym doors came the Gentlemen. They walked in a straight line, emotionless. The crowd, paralytic in shock, did not notice them making their way to the stage.

Except for Principal Wiener. Fearing one of them might be his son in disguise, he began to run towards the performers as they walked on stage.

Then, absolute chaos broke out in the gymnasium. Paralysis became terror, and teens screamed in confusion, zipped in every direction, and trampled those who got in the way of their exit.

Someone tipped over the snack table, awakening a sense of alertness in Coach Kumin. He began to grab random kids, shake them by the shoulders, and tell them to "cool the fuck down."

Jenny slipped off her heels and ran over to the small set of bleachers lining the wall opposite the toppled snack table. She crawled under the bleachers, watching the chaos through the gap between benches.

She knew fleeing the gym was no safer than staying. She would scout out the situation and take the time to formulate a plan.

Brittany Beverly and Matt Brady stood dumbstruck on stage, blood coating their color-coordinated outfits. Matt no longer felt like the coolest guy in Barbara Falls. Matt wanted to run home to his mommy, cry in her lap, and sleep in her bed, like he had in his youth, when he was so scared of the boogeyman in his closet that he would pee his pajamas. He felt her loving kiss on his forehead as a dampness spread across the front of his dress pants.

The brainless Gentlemen marched on stage and reached for their instruments. Their eyes stared into the black abyss of nothingness, their souls long since departed, their bodies now mere vessels.

Brittany and Matt stood in front of Bernard Hook's bass guitar. To embrace his musical weapon, Hook mindlessly threw Brittany out of the way.

What little balance Brittany had in her seven-inch heels was thrown to the curb. More precisely, it was thrown into the gaping hole on-stage, as was Brittany's head, which met a sharp splinter of plywood sticking out towards the sky. Her shield of makeup was no match against the shard of wood, which punctured her throat and severed her voice box.

She never got the chance to give her acceptance speech. Instead, the last thing out of her mouth was a rush of bloody vomit, which gave Corey Jones' face its first shower in over a week. As Brittany Beverly choked out her last vomitous breath, all her valley girl cronies wished she could've met a *cuter* demise.

The splash of prom queen blood reawakened Corey's respiratory system, and he sucked in a whole ounce of chunky gore, lodging his throat closed. Viscera had blocked his entire windpipe. Each attempt at inhalation accomplished nothing but further panic in Corey. His water gun fell to the ground as he wrapped his arms around his throat.

Corey's vision began to narrow. *Boy,* he thought. *What a shitty prank.* He then collapsed to the ground, dead as a doornail or any other subgenre of nail.

"You son of a bitch!" the wet Matt Brady cried. He shed three very masculine tears at the sight of his girlfriend being impaled to death, and then set his sights on the man responsible, Bernard Hook. He swung his quarterback arm into Hook's face. The bassist took the hit like a punching bag, bouncing back to his original position like rubber.

"What the…" Matt was cut off by Hook bringing down his hand and strumming all four strings of his bass guitar. The noise blew out of his Marshall amp with violence. Paul Score and Steven Sylvian followed his lead, ferociously strumming open chords and slamming crash cymbals.

The ear-shattering noise shook the gymnasium. Strands of rope lights across the room flickered on and off. The wooden, sparkly stars hanging from the ceiling began to fall from the sky. The noise drowned out the students' screams, but not their mind-melting fear.

Matt heard a shout from the side of the stage. He

swung his head towards the sound.

Principal Wiener was pointing a handgun right at him.

"I said… duck, idiot!" Wiener shouted.

Matt did as he was told and hit the deck. Wiener unloaded three rounds into Bernard Hook's face. Two hit him in the temple, and the last exploded his left eye. Fresh bloodstains painted Hook's amp, but the man's head popped back into place.

He never missed a note. The band's Satanic dirge went on as planned.

Matt screamed in disbelief. Football practice had not prepared him for this.

Jimbo and Abigail Williams were the first two to make it to the exit. Jimbo dragged Abigail like a rag doll to the double doors. He wasn't going to fucking die tonight. His life was far too important.

He took hold of one of the double doors and swung it open with all his might. Waiting outside was merely more horror: a masked man with a handheld, gas-powered garden tiller. He yanked on the pull start, and four rows of blades thrust towards his chest.

Jimbo thought quickly and valorously, throwing Abigail towards the killer and shutting the gym door behind her. The masked man's tiller met Abigail's face, shredding her nose and lips and ruining any chance she had of professionally playing the trumpet.

She screamed one final time. She died as she lived, ignored by everyone around her.

Rachel Severinsen ran on stage, doing the opposite of most of her classmates. She ran to her lover's corpse, still soaked in the class president's blood and vomit, and collapsed into hoarse sobs over him. Even the least likable of humans are, occasionally, capable of choosing love over fear, anxiety, and hatred.

Principal Wiener tried another strategy, shooting out Hook's bass amp. Sparks shot from the amp and it lost power, leaving Hook to strum a bass without amplification. The brain-numbing noise turned down one notch.

Just enough for Rachel to hear the robotic growling coming from underneath the stage.

As Wiener took potshots at Paul Score's guitar amp, a mechanical dog leapt through the hole in the wooden stage and onto Rachel, tearing out her throat and decapitating her in one fell swoop.

The head rolled towards the upturned snack table, and Fido, as he was trained, went to go fetch it. The dog gobbled up strings of gore hanging from Rachel's eviscerated neck with ferocious glee.

Wiener's lead wad finally shot in the right direction, hitting the cord plugged into Score's amp and blowing it to pieces. Two of the three Gentlemen were now playing their funereal tune to no one.

Jimbo ran away from the gym doors, as did the handful of promgoers who saw the masked man waiting for them outside. Jimbo ran towards the bleachers, where he heard someone yelling his name.

He peeked through the slits of the pews and spied Jenny. She signaled for him to hide alongside her with a movement of her hand. His heart pumping with twice the ferocity it did during his two-minute sex sessions, he did not deny the invitation.

"Let's just stay here until the time is right," Jenny whispered as he crouched next to her.

"What?" Jimbo asked, the crashing of cymbals still polluting the air.

She repeated her sentence. He repeated his.

"We have to get *out* of here, Deborah!" Dick Wong-Dick yelled to his love. She stood motionless, transfixed by the sight of her bandmates getting shot in the head.

Wong-Dick grabbed Deborah by both arms and shook her.

"I love you, Deborah!"

Deborah snapped out of it.

"We have to run! I'm too pretty to die!" Deborah yelled.

"Deborah, in case this is it… kiss me." Faced with the prospect of dying never having kissed a girl,

Wong-Dick's confidence had increased tenfold.

Deborah had long forgotten about making Wong-Dick fall in love with her to help her band achieve fame. It seemed stardom was simply not in the cards for The Gentlemen. Their deck seemed stacked with jokers… and grim reapers.

All of her dreams deceased, Deborah nodded, and, while crying, shut her eyes and moved her face towards his.

Wong-Dick's heart leapt out of its heart socket. He closed his eyes and slowly moved towards Deborah's luscious lips.

As they met, Wong-Dick thought the kiss felt strangely sharp. Wooden, even. As he sensually licked in and around her mouth, he felt the poking of splinters on his tongue.

Strange, he thought in Korean. *This isn't at all what I thought it would feel like.*

He opened his eyes, only to find his tongue had been embracing a large, glittery wooden star, which had fallen from the ceiling and thrust itself through Deborah's face. Her mouth hung grotesquely ajar, a bloody point poking from between two sets of dismantled teeth.

Deborah seized slightly. Her eyes showed a dim awareness of approaching death, which, morbidly, enhanced her beauty up until the moment she voided her bowels and died.

Wong-Dick stared at the scene before him, a blood-red cherry on the sundae of shit that was his sad, sad life. He dropped to his knees in tears, his puke-orange pants splashing into a pool of innards.

Principal Wiener had shot down all of Steven Sylvian's cymbals, opting to take them out with his pistol instead of climbing on stage and moving them a couple feet away from the brainless drum automaton. The Gentlemen continued to play their instruments, but now, no noise came from the crime scene of a stage.

Instead, the gym was filled once more with the melodious sounds of teens fearing for their lives.

Now, Wiener had to find his son. He looked around the stage but saw nothing. He must not have entered the gym with the band... which meant he was somewhere else.

That's when the sound of someone getting his throat slit with a garden tiller came barreling towards his ears.

Wiener shifted his head towards the double doors of the gym and saw the origin of the sound: Sam Berry getting his throat slit by a masked man with a garden tiller.

It was the first time Wiener had seen his son for ten years. He did what any father would do after such a long absence. He pulled a flamethrower from his backpack, ignited it, and pointed it towards his demon spawn.

"Benjamin!" Wiener's cry rang out through the gym.

The killer was enjoying scalping Sam Berry's date with his gardening tool when he heard the cries of his father. He shoved the girl to the ground, spilling her shockingly normal-sized brain onto the gym floor. A smile wrapped around his face.

"Daddy!" Benjamin whooped.

He began to walk towards the man who gave him life, determined to now give him death. It was the prom attendees' first chance to escape the gym, and Mr. Stannaker, Coach Kumin, Brad Fahey, and his date wasted no time, running out into the foyer.

Wiener pulled the trigger on his flamethrower, sending a five-foot-long spray of glorious yellow and red across the gymnasium and immediately torching "Piggy" Donner like a stuck pig at a roast.

In under thirty seconds, Kimberly lost all the weight she had dreamed of losing her entire life. Unfortunately, before she could even get a chance to star in a diet infomercial, she was six lean, mean pounds of ash.

Mrs. Poughkeepsie ran towards the exit, squawking at the top of her lungs. She kept her eyes to the ground, dipping and dodging around the bodies and internal organs strewn in piles across the gymnasium floor.

She had obviously failed at bringing God back to Barbara Falls High. *This must be the end of days, as the Good Book promised,* she thought. But why was *she* being punished? Where were the cavalcade of angels, trumpets in hand, there to lead her by the hand to her eternity in everlasting bliss? She would have to put in a little complaint to God about their timeliness when this was all over and done with!

Lost in thought and sure-footed concentration, Poughkeepsie snapped back into reality when she felt a huge, calloused hand grab her by her neck paunches. She felt herself being lifted from the ground and turned her eyes towards her assailant.

It was no angel come down from above to save her. It was a masked man, and the evil in his eyes was far fiercer than that of any misbehaving teenager. She let out a squeak, her avian call now lodged in her constricted throat.

The killer ripped loose the binoculars around Poughkeepsie's neck and thrust them deep into her ajar mouth, shattering rows of teeth and sending them flying down her struggling windpipe. Gore ran from her maw as the killer continued to push, tearing through the back of her throat and pushing the bloodied binoculars cleanly out the other side.

"Father! I can *see* you!" the killer screamed.

He pushed the nearly-expired teacher to the ground. She was met there by Fido, who dug its iron teeth into her stomach and feasted on her appendix and large intestine.

Cheg Larson looked to his left and saw the bassist of a shitty new wave band ooze blood from the three bullet holes in his head onto the dead body of Barbara Falls High's prom queen. He looked to his right and saw a nerd desperately try to get his shoe unstuck from the cheerleader brain he had accidentally stepped in. He looked straight ahead as a pillar of flame rocketed towards meek Mr. Doughty and melted his flesh like a stick of butter in the microwave.

A tear ran down the left cheek of Cheg Larson's butt-ugly face. The first smile that face had ever known shined as brightly as the twinkling string lights falling and penetrating deeply into Mr. Doughty's conflagrating body.

He had waited his entire life for just this moment. He lifted his jean-jacketed arms to the sky, outstretched the pointer and pinky fingers of each hand, and screamed at the top of his lungs.

"This… is *so…* METAL!" He banged his head and embraced the amazing moment.

Three centimeters of blood had pooled up throughout the gymnasium. It was the largest display of solidarity the senior class of Barbara Falls had ever shown. For the first time, a Sandy van Thorpe was on the same standing as a Brittany

Beverly. It was cute and incredibly icky.

"Now's our chance," Jenny Hibiscus whispered to Jimbo, who shivered in fear next to her. The killer was now fifteen feet from the gym doors, swinging his tiller back and forth to intimidate the fiery Wiener working his way towards him.

"Jenny, I'm scared." Jimbo grabbed Jenny's shoulder, fear enveloping his large, green eyes. Jenny stared at him for a second.

"Shut your big, fat pussy mouth, Jimbo," she said. She leapt up and began to run towards the double doors. Jimbo swallowed his fear and followed behind her.

Without missing a step, Jenny scooped up the squashed cheerleader brain laying on the gym floor like a fumbled football.

"What are you doing?" Jimbo shouted.

"Just in case," she replied.

They slipped by the distracted killer and into the foyer. The main entrance boarded shut, their only option was the far back door. They saw Stannaker, Cumin, Brad and his date running down the long hallway to get there.

Jimbo and Jenny stood alone in the school's entranceway, their only company the shredded body of Abigail Williams.

Looking at her filleted face, Jimbo felt a twinge of guilt for the first time. It was because of him this girl was dead. He had been the last person she ever talked to, but he couldn't remember what she had said. His focus had instead been on her chest.

As he reminisced, he realized, again, despite everything, he was staring right at her boobs.

Oh my God, Jimbo McKinney thought. *I think I'm an asshole.*

This stunning realization kicked Jimbo's mind into overdrive. What if this entire night was happening to show him he needed to change? God works in mysterious ways, right? Everything happens for a reason, and he would use this opportunity to become a better person. Hell, he would give up everything, and go volunteer in Thailand to help all the starving Africans not die of AIDS.

"Where's your van?" Jenny asked.

"I don't know! That fucking cunt Jane stole it!" Jimbo yelled.

"Oh, God... okay, we'll follow behind the others. Stay a ways back. That way, we know what's ahead," Jenny said.

"Just get me out of here alive, Jenny," Jimbo cried.

"I'll get myself out of here... you're just collateral."

Jenny ran down the long corridor of B.F. High, cheerleader brain dripping goo all the way. Jimbo inserted his tail between his legs and followed.

Chapter 17

Blackness.

Crazy Jane loved blackness. She had painted her room black to match her Bauhaus and Cure posters, draped the space in blackout curtains to keep the wretched sun out.

The blackness she found herself in now was less comfortable. What was her head propped up against? Why were her legs bent like this? Where was she?

It all flooded back to her. The giant, gelatin creature. Principal Wiener's story. Being told to look outside… and after that?

Judging by the throbbing pain in the back of her head, Wiener must have knocked her out and put her somewhere. A closet, maybe? But why? She didn't wake up dead, so he must've wanted her alive. Was he trying to protect her? And his secret along with her?

She crunched her elbow against the sheet metal her head rested on, again and again, until the door busted open. She spilled out onto the floor with a loud *oof*.

Wiener's office was dark, and she was alone. The file labeled 'KILLER' still sat neatly on his desk. Jane felt an urge to open up the file and gobble up more details on Wiener's son, but more pressing questions flooded her pounding head.

What time was it? Who's still alive? And what's left of them?

Jane opened Wiener's office door and tiptoed through the main office into the foyer. On the ground was the dead body of one of her classmates, a girl she had never talked to. It appeared she'd never get the chance: based on the state of her face, her prom date had been a cheese grater.

The sounds of horrible screams and painful death reverberated through the gym doors. Jane decided the place to go was *not* the dance hall.

Someone had boarded up the front door, leaving the long hallway as her only exit. A trail of gory fluid traveled down the corridor, perhaps from one of the syphilitic creatures she met outside. This didn't leave her feeling confident, but it was her only option.

Taking one long, deep breath, she put one foot in front of the other until she found herself walking down the ominous corridor.

Blackness.

As the seven-foot-high slug creature with a vagina for a face devoured Brad Fahey whole, disintegrating his being into vomit proteins, all poor Brad could see, hear, or think was blackness.

His date, dismayed at the sudden turn of events, buried her crying head into Mr. Stannaker's side nook. Stannaker comforted her, just hoping the beautiful girl would not ask him what in God's name they were going to do, because he had no fucking idea.

"What in God's name are we going to do?!" Brad Fahey's date cried.

Coach Kumin had the only answer. He kicked in the nearest classroom door and ran inside. Stannaker and the girl backed away from the encroaching monster, whose scab-covered gelatin flesh now stretched the length of the entire hallway. The lumbering yellow monolith of filth towered above the puny humans with gooey authority.

"What are you doing, Coach? He'll corner us in there!" Stannaker yelled.

Coach emerged, carrying a desk. "Not if we fight back! Take *this!*"

He threw the desk at the creature and ran back into the classroom for another. The creature absorbed the tossed desk like a sumo wrestler playing paintball, sucking its weight in and depositing the desk with nary a rumble. Its stomach gurgled with mucus.

"Coach, it's useless!" Stannaker said.

"Don't give up that easy, Stannaker! It can't take our beatings forever!" Coach came out, threw another desk at the slug, and retreated to the classroom. The creature responded by sending a fire hose's spray of yellow and green chunks all over Stannaker and the girl.

The girl screamed until her brain turned to mush. Stannaker didn't have the chance. The vomit rocketed down his agape mouth, liquefying his throat and spinal cord to stew. For eight seconds, he wondered if the questionable, predatory decisions he had made throughout his life would send him to Hell, then he slipped into an eternity of emptiness.

Jenny and Jimbo turned the corner into the hallway. They could do nothing but watch as the blob lumbered towards Stannaker and the girl and stepped into their bodies.

One second, they were there. The next, they were absorbed into the gelatin of the creature.

Jimbo froze, mortified at the sight before him. It had to be his imagination, but it looked like the thing rolling down the hallway in a pile of its own goo was getting bigger as it moved towards them! The crawling wall of jaundiced flesh spurted pus from the torn scabs littering its body. Its only recognizable feature was a diseased slit, six inches across, wheezing, coughing, and dribbling vomit onto itself as it slid down the hallway.

Jimbo screamed. He tried to run in the opposite direction, but his feet refused to move. He was powerless, his masculinity shriveled up like a dried-out grape.

Jenny pitched the cheerleader brain right at the blob. It widened its rank opening and the brain slipped between its exposed oral labia, sucked right into its inner gelatin.

All was silent for a second, save Coach Kumin tearing apart the adjacent classroom. Then, a harsh screeching erupted from the horrible being. Its entire mass shook back and forth, quaking the hallway walls with fury.

Jenny and Jimbo toppled to the ground as the screeching became more and more unbearable. They both clutched their ears in pain.

Crazy Jane approached from the foyer and saw Jimbo and Jenny Hibiscus fall over. She took a long sigh of relief. *Somebody* was still alive who wasn't Jimbo McKinney.

Then, the harsh death knells reached her eardrums. She was thrown to the ground, the intense vibrations dismantling her balance.

Inside the classroom, the rumbling threw Coach Kumin, desk in hands, off balance. He tumbled over and cracked his head against a stack of copies of *Things Fall Apart*, knocking him unconscious.

A black pillar grew inside the horror's gelatinous insides. As the pillar became larger, the creature's skin discolored from the inside out. The screeching reached a fever pitch; Jenny's eardrums felt close to bursting.

Something else burst first. One of the monster's scabs, a ripe pimple on its lower half, popped and spewed jet-black pus onto the floor. Then another. And another. Before long, the creature was springing more leaks than a ship docked at Pearl Harbor.

Black sludge spread across the floor as the monster slowly deflated. Its screeching died down to a lowly whine. The sea of sludge washed over Jenny and Jimbo like the evening tide, staining Jenny's navy blue dress and severely diminishing its resale value.

Jane was up on her feet before they were, and she rushed over, helping them up. The leaking being in front of them was now only about a foot and a half tall, its yellowed skin stretched out and wrinkled beyond repair.

"Oh my god, Jane!" Jenny wrapped her arms around her, striking Jane by surprise. "I'm so glad someone else is alive."

Jimbo pouted in anger. "Well, if it isn't the bitch

that..."

"Jimbo, the ladies are talking," Jenny said without looking in his direction. Jimbo stayed silent, his ego and manhood now as severely deflated as the creature.

"Principal Wiener knocked me out and locked me in his closet," Jane said. "Jenny, it sounds like Hell in that gym."

"Hell wouldn't know what hit it if it went in there," Jenny said. "It's the worst thing I've seen in my life, and earlier tonight, I held my boyfriend's dead remains in my hands after seeing Leslie Deakins' naked, mutilated body."

Jane never thought much of people, preferring the moody and macabre escape of music and film. Staring into Jenny's eyes touched a deeper place. The depths of human suffering can never be summed up in a mere song. To see it in its purest form, you had to go to the source.

She hugged Jenny back, the first time she'd hugged anyone since she last laid her hands on her mother in sixth grade.

"I'm so sorry, Jenny," she whispered in her ear.

"I've... lost everyone tonight," Jenny quietly answered. "Jeremy... Sarah... Rothschild..."

"Wait, Rothschild and Sarah are dead?!" Jimbo cried.

Jenny nodded. Jimbo dropped to his knees and

pounded the ground, splashing his fists in a puddle of black sludge. He was as sad as someone who had forgotten to ask about the well-being of two of his best friends for over ten minutes could be.

By now, the blob creature had completely disintegrated. All that remained was a thin film of cheesecloth skin, a gooey cheerleader brain, and a pile of teeth.

"How did you know that brain would kill it?" Jimbo asked from the ground.

"Jeremy taught me it was allergic to death," Jenny answered. "He taught me from beyond the grave."

Jane had a feeling she had underrated Jenny Hibiscus. She assumed everyone in the school was a worthless idiot, especially those who hung around Rothschild and Jimbo. Jenny had smiled and exchanged pleasantries with her in Mr. Stannaker's English class, but she thought she was just being fake. Maybe, just maybe, she was wrong.

"Well, enough talking, guys," Jane said. "Let's get out of here."

"That reminds me..." Jimbo said, getting up off the ground and wading through black sludge to get to Jane.

"Your van's at Hamburger Heaven," she interrupted. "Hopefully."

"What do you mean..." Jimbo said.

"Let's go!" Jenny said.

They worked their way through hills of blackened, mucky pus, then ran the rest of the way to the cafetorium. Inside, Jenny was careful not to look at the stage, knowing the cruel work of theater which lay beyond the curtains.

They made it to the back door and pushed it open. Hamburger Heaven was only a few minutes' walk away… as long as nothing got in their way first.

As they jogged towards the front of the building, a small, gray four-door, headlights blaring, roared into the parking lot. The mysterious car pulled right in front of them.

Jimbo nearly peed himself at the sight. He stared in horror at the car. What could it be now? The killer's distant cousin? A vampiric robot cop? Sexy Chinese twins? Nothing could surprise him after everything he'd seen tonight.

The window of the car slowly cranked open, revealing a normal-looking man.

"Excuse me, you all look like you're in a hurry, but do any of you happen to know a Jeremy Vernon?" the man asked.

The words stabbed Jenny Hibiscus' heart like a switchblade.

The stranger was of late middle-age, with short, straw-brown hair and glowing green eyes peeking from behind thick glasses. A light goatee enriched his pleasant face, along with a half-smile that didn't mask the look of concern etched in his eyes.

Why does he look so familiar? Jenny asked herself as she stared.

Then it hit her. He looked almost exactly like an older Jeremy.

"Did you say Jeremy Vernon?" she asked.

"Yes... I'm his uncle. I don't know how to say this, but I have a feeling in the pit of my stomach that he's in terrible danger," the man said.

Jenny's wall of strength collapsed under a wrecking ball of emotion. Tears streamed down her face. She turned away, trying to hide from everyone's judging eyes.

Mark Vernon, however, had never developed judging eyes. He switched off the car and got out. He walked over to Jenny and, without a word, embraced her in a hug.

Jenny wrapped her arms tight around the man, who had a physique similar to Jeremy's except that it was different in almost every way.

"He's dead, isn't he?" Mark quietly asked Jenny. Her sobs answered for her.

"I hate to interrupt this touching moment, but there's a serial killer in the gymnasium. We need to get out of here now!" Jimbo said.

"A serial killer?" Mark asked. His mind flashed back to the bloody visions at work that very morning. "Was he from a... mental hospital?"

"I didn't get a chance to interview him," Jimbo answered.

It's exactly like my visions, Mark thought. He couldn't believe it. His clairvoyance had returned. But he was too late. His poor, talented nephew was dead, killed by some psychopath.

Mark believed that everything happened for a reason, as many people without a grasp of the sadistic board game of life do. He knew his visions had brought him all the way to Barbara Falls for a reason, and with his nephew gone, he had a feeling it had something to do with this group of teenagers and the madman inside their school.

He broke his hold on Jenny. "I'm Mark Vernon," he said. "Jeremy's uncle, like I said."

"Jenny Hibiscus. I was Jeremy's girlfriend... until he became a skeleton."

"For fuck's sake, don't care. Time to leave!" Jimbo asked.

"Jimbo's right," Mark said. "Everybody in my car. We've got to book it and fast."

"Wait, how..." Jimbo was ignored as everyone piled into Mark's sedan. He reluctantly followed.

"We'll go to the police station. Tell them to bring everything they've got," Mark said as he slammed the driver side door.

"They already have," Jenny said. "They're all dead."

"Then we'll go to the next town over. And if they're dead, on to the next. And if they're dead, God damn it, we'll go to Vancouver and bring down all the mounties they've got!"

He put the keys in the ignition and turned them.

Nothing. He tried again. And again. But the car was dead.

"Damn, I must've run out of gas back in Nashville," Mark said.

"If only my van was…" Jimbo started.

"Hamburger Heaven," Jane finished. "Let's go."

"I never thought I'd say this, Jane," Mark said. "But I can't say Hamburger Heaven sounds very appetizing right now."

"Trust me… we won't be eating," Jane said, getting out of the car.

"Wait, how does he know our…" Jimbo started. No one listened.

Outside, the crisp wind grew stronger, colder, more climactic.

Blackness.

Charred, blackened remains of teachers and students coagulated on the blood-soaked wood flooring of the high school gymnasium. The smell of toasty, hellish death hung in the air.

The sweltering temperature burst bulbs on the string lights across the gym ceiling, setting strands on fire and lighting an unholy blaze above the horrible scene.

Sandy van Thorpe and the prom committee's glittery stars rained down onto the students below, gruesomely ripping through the chests of those unlucky enough to still be living, setting ablaze their internal organs and roasting them from the inside out.

One of these stars had dug deep into the head of Paul Score, tragically mussing up his orange crab-claw haircut and turning his head into a glittery jack-o-lantern. He continued to play thunderous, unplugged chords to an audience of corpses.

Principal Wiener's disheveled suit was now more sweat than cotton, but he kept the flamethrower in his hands running. He would do so until it ran out of gas or his son ran out of life.

Benjamin sidestepped the flame again and again, waiting to sink a well-timed slash into his father's self-righteous face. The unbearable heat fused the rough pigskin of his wrestling mask with the skin below, but the pain only swelled Benjamin's confidence, knowing it was bringing him closer with El Cazador and his dark lord.

Fido ran back and forth, chowing down joyously on the insides of the dead. Its current meal was a member of the Barbara Falls drama squad. She was a little stringy, but the dog didn't mind.

The few still alive were out of options. The double doors to the gym were bedazzled in flame. The skeleton hands of the last couple who had tried to escape them still grasped the door handles.

This left Matt Brady with very little hope, and he hid under the bleachers with a couple drama geeks he had never talked to before. They all huddled, cried together, and prayed for a miracle. Matt still wore his Prom King crown, the last remnant of his old life.

Dick Wong-Dick remained collapsed on the ground. He'd been blubbering since the death of Deborah Moyet, letting the waves of blood wash over him and laying low enough to avoid the rocketing heat of Wiener's flame. Wong-Dick had long accepted death, hoping he had earned enough karma in this life to be reborn as an attractive prince with impressive girth.

"Benjamin, it's over! Give up!" Principal Wiener yelled to his son. He pushed forward with his flamethrower, sidestepping Benjamin into a corner. Wiener grinned. The boy had no chance.

"Daddy, it's never over when you put your faith in the Lord," he said, smiling. "Lord Satan, that is."

"I'll always love you, Benjamin," Wiener said. "Now *die*!"

Wiener ran his son into the corner and cleansed him with a hot shower. A really hot one.

Benjamin's blood-drenched trench coat went up first, then his mask, then his entire body. The murderous killer ran around in circles, holding his garden tiller high. He stopped, dropped, and rolled, dropping his weapon and rolling it towards the principal. He stopped, dropped, and rolled until he stopped dropping and rolling and dropped his head to the ground.

Principal Forrest Wiener stared at the bonfire that was his son, at the chaos around him, at the few crying, screaming students who weren't part of the large pile of blood and ashes. Wiener smiled. There had been casualties, but he could rest easy knowing he had prevented a true tragedy at Barbara Falls High.

He dropped the burnt-out flamethrower to the ground and grabbed the red-hot tiller lying at his feet. If the fire had not already done in his son, the garden tool sure would.

"You're wrong, Benjamin," he said. "Satan's no match for Father."

He yanked on the tiller's pull-start to bring the device to life, then slowly brought it down towards his son's face. But before it could make gooey contact, a razor-sharp pain inflamed Wiener's side and thrust him to the ground.

It was Fido. The digital dog dug its metallic snout into Wiener's side, slurping up his gallbladder and swallowing it whole. Wiener screamed as the gnashing continued.

Then, as if from Heaven, a burning comet of light dug itself into the back of Fido. A pitiful yelp escaped the dog's mouth. It let loose Wiener's organ from its mouth, then collapsed to the floor with a plop.

Wiener ambled away from the dog. A wooden star, flaming with glittering aplomb, was wedged into the gym floor. It had sliced the robo-dog cleanly in half.

He shuffled to his hands and knees, one hand covering the spurting wound in his side. He looked around for the garden tiller. He had to finish what he started. But where was the damn thing?

Wiener looked towards his son's body.

It was gone.

"Jesus Christ..." Wiener muttered.

"He's not here right now, can I take a message?" A voice behind him laughed.

Wiener spun around. His son, still engulfed head-to-toe in flames, stood right behind him. Through the fire and mask melted to his face, Wiener could still see a mangled smile.

Principal Wiener let loose one final, primal scream. His son rose the tiller to the sky and thrust it through his father's face, turning it into a finely tilled field of face meat.

Blood drizzled down Wiener's clothes. The outermost slices of face drooped down and splattered onto the gym floor, leaving only a mangled, three-inch slice in the middle.

The killer cackled maniacally as his father's dead body slumped to the ground. He threw the weapon down and patted out the patches of unruly flame clinging to his clothes, then took a moment to look around him and admire his masterwork.

"Here, little piggies! Who's next?" The killer circled the gym, yearning for more murder. It was all that drove him, the single activity that kept him engaged and wishing to live. Existence was meaningless, empty, futile, except that it gave him more time to kill.

On the other side of the gym, Cheg Larson, tears in his eyes, smile on his face, raised his hand to the sky.

"Kill *me*, Mr. Killer!" he yelled. "These last ten minutes have been the most *metal* moments of my life! Fuck ever trying to top them! End me!"

"Your wish is my command, Jean Jacket," the killer said, approaching Cheg. "Not many boys your age are this... sensible."

Cheg outstretched his arms and closed his eyes, ready for his hero to heave him to Hell.

And then the ceiling fell.

The aged infrastructure of the gym collapsed

under the stress of fire and limited public school budgets. Chunks of building crushed the makeshift stage, ruining what was left of Paul Score's hairdo and demolishing thousands of dollars of musical equipment.

The weakened foundation spread across the fiery ceiling, sending cement and asphalt to the ground below. The weight buckled the bleachers downwards, pummeling aluminum through the skulls of Matt Brady and the drama geeks, crushing them into bloodied dust.

Before long, all that was left of the prom was a pile of rubble.

It was a genocide of such brutal proportions that no one could possibly survive. Absolutely no one. Not a chance in Hell.

Chapter 18

Jimbo McKinney had walked the two blocks between Barbara Falls High and Hamburger Heaven more times than he could count. He would go after school, during Mrs. Poughkeepsie's class, for a quick Cheesy Beefy Heaven Breakfast combo right after waking up.

Never before had the walk been a battle against all-encompassing fear.

Jimbo tensed up at each building they passed, expecting an asphyxiating blob monster to lurch out at them. Every shadow was a killer, each tree a murderer. He even felt himself being followed by Abigail Williams' ghost, desperate for revenge.

In short, he was being a fucking pussy. Jimbo beat up pussies. He wanted to punch himself in the gut, give himself a wedgie, throw himself into a locker. The dissolution of his manhood was, to him, the biggest tragedy of the night.

The group in front of him walked quickly towards the burger joint. They stayed cautious, but did not want to give the horrors behind them the chance to catch up.

"I think we're the only ones left alive," Jane said. Inside the school, Coach Kumin woke up from his literary coma, as if to prove her wrong.

"Well, that's better than no one being alive," Mark Vernon replied. He walked in front alongside Jenny Hibiscus.

"And we'll stay alive, too," Jenny continued. "Think about it… we'll all go on a beach holiday after this. Hawaii… Florida… or…"

"Petite Mustique Island in St. Vincent and the Grenadines," Mark finished.

Jenny looked at him. "I've always wanted to go there."

"We will." Mark smiled.

He looked at Jenny. While being in a town full of corpses hung over them like mistletoe over a door on Christmas, it was nice to have someone to talk to and calm down with. Mark definitely understood what his nephew had seen in Jenny. It was really a shame he had to go and get murdered.

"So, what's our plan again?" Jane asked. "And why shouldn't I just book it home and hope for the best?"

"We're safer together," Jenny said. "And we're out of dead people to throw."

"We'll use the payphone at Hamburger Heaven

to call the police. The National Guard, even," Mark said. "Then, we'll grab Jimbo's van and get as far away from here as we can possibly get."

"Thanks for thinking of a plan, Mark," Jenny said softly.

"I feel like it's my duty now," he said, turning to look her in the eyes. "In honor of Jeremy."

"Jeremy was..." Jenny started.

"Special," Mark said.

"Exactly."

"More than special. It's hard to explain. He may have kept things from you, but that's only because he loved you."

"It was him who warned us all about the murderer. He saved our lives," Jenny whispered.

"That's just how Jeremy was. Trust me, I know. I haven't seen him in almost a decade."

"You're right," Jenny said. "It's just so comforting to talk to..."

"Someone," Mark finished. They stopped and looked at each other. "Wow, this just keeps..."

"Happening," Jenny said, as she fell in love with Mark Vernon.

Hamburger Heaven loomed in the distance, unaware it would be the setting for the night's grand finale.

A desert. A hot one.

A lone man, a keffiyeh shielding his face from the oppressive desert sun, rode a camel down hump after hump of sand. His covering once shielded his face from the rivulets of sweat, but the moisture had won out in the end.

From what the man remembered, he was born traveling the desert, and he would die traveling the desert. He felt this end was not far off. The icy cold hand of Death seemed a welcome reprieve from the mesmerizing sun. He longed to shake that hand.

His only companions were his trusty camel and the large rocks that littered the wide-open landscape. Stumbling across another lost soul out here was a fantasy he'd left behind long ago.

But what was that, up ahead? Squinting his eyes, he could see what looked like a small lake in the distance. Could it be? Or was it the desert playing yet another cruel trick?

His steed soon approached the body of water, and the man's eyes widened. His eyes had not deceived him. The gleaming liquid sparkled with the sun's reflection. He dismounted his camel and shambled to the pool.

Collapsing onto the wet sand, the man plunged his sun-fried hands deep into the water. The rush of liquid over his limbs sent shivers of ecstasy across his body. He splashed his face repeatedly and invited his animal to do the same.

His eyes clenched in pleasure, the man did not notice the two robed arms ascending from out of the water until they were wrapped around his neck.

He was being pulled under the surface. Deeper. And deeper.

Opening his eyes in the sea-blue wonderland, he found himself staring eye-to-eye with another man. A green and black wrestling mask obscured the man's grizzled face.

The traveler let in a deep breath of air. To his surprise, he could breathe perfectly fine in this underwater oasis.

"Hola, mi aprendiz. Though hard times have befallen you, you must not lose sight of your mission. The end goal is near, and you must finish the job *en el nombre de Satanás,"* the masked man said.

El Cazador. Visions of the past thrust themselves into the traveler's mind. Of course. The man was his savior long ago. In the time before the desert.

"This is no desert," the man continued. "Beware of His mirages He forces on your mind. *En el mundo real,* the time is near for you to let loose *las fuerzas del Infierno."*

I am weak, the man thought. *I know not where to look, nor what to do.*

"A monolithic creature of slime. Cow's flesh shaped into patties. A man with powers much like your own. These are your tools. With them, the world will soon be ours. Now, wake from your burning slumber, *mijo,* and complete your mission."

The masked man sunk deeper and deeper into the bottomless water. The wanderer reached out, but was rocketed upwards towards whence he came. As his body broke the surface of the lake, the desert melted away, replaced by darkness.

And a single fist rose from amongst the smoldering rubble of the Barbara Falls High gymnasium.

From the back exit, Coach Kumin booked it out of the school with intense fixation. He wanted to get home, pour himself four or five cups of vodka, and fall asleep on the couch. Tell Mrs. Coach all about his hell of a night in the morning. To think, she was probably sleeping right now! As he was running for his life! That bitch better not complain about his drinking tomorrow!

The coach ran with such single-minded ferocity that he didn't even notice the other half of the school had caved in, ignoring the smoldering ruins as one would a televised WNBA game.

Behind him, the killer had dislodged most of his body from the debris. He pulled his right leg out of the rubble. It faced the wrong way, so he pivoted the bone back into place with a loud crunch. Good as new.

As he brushed himself off, he heard a whimper

coming from the gym rubble.

"Fido, boy!" the killer yelled. "You're still alive!"

He pushed chunks of plaster and asbestos aside to unearth his monstrous pet. There was not much left of Fido: only the front pair of roller-skate wheels remained, and its shiny, metallic coat was dusty and unkempt. The dog's tongue lolled from its vicious mouth, and a glassy visage of pain shone from its eyes.

"It's okay, boy. Death is nothing to fear," the killer whispered, cradling his beloved dog in his hands. "*El Cazador* will lead you to the next plane of existence. You have served Him well."

The touching moment was interrupted by the approach of an oozing, bubbling vaginal slug. The killer looked up at the deranged specter of gelatinous flesh ambling atop the gymnasium of rubble and smiled.

A monolithic creature of slime. The first of the three prophecies, he thought. *Gracias, El Cazador.*

Still cradling the front half of Fido in his arms, he stood up from the rubble and walked towards the creature without fear. As the substance of sewage and slime opened its blistered labia and splattered him in a revolting shower of vomit, he felt no pain, even when his barbecued flesh started to sizzle in the evening air. And when the creature surrounded him whole to devour his entire essence, all Benjamin Wiener felt was a surge of excitement and an all-encompassing devotion to his unholy God.

Soon, the creature recoiled, shrieking, from the hunk of pure depravity it had attempted to feed upon, but it was too late. The killer's eyes sunk back towards his brain as his entire body convulsed in a seizure of evil. The creature's gelatinous mass melted into hellish liquid and poured itself into each one of the killer's orifices. Gonorrheal slime overtook Benjamin's eyelids, his ear canals, his oral cavity, merged with the blackness within, and began to glow with the vivacity of an exploding star.

The sprinting Coach Kumin stopped in the street, as he noticed the sun was rising behind him. *The sun... was I knocked out all night?* he asked himself.

He turned towards the sunrise, excited for the first moment of beauty he had seen all night.

Instead, one glimpse at the evil, fluorescent glow expanding amidst the rubble of the high school gymnasium popped Coach Kumin's eyeballs like microwaved potatoes and melted the skin from his bones in three seconds flat. His skeleton, still clothed in a blue tracksuit and Reebok Reverse Jams, remained standing, transfixed, in the middle of Main Street.

The vitreous-melting glow cooled and the remains of Barbara Falls High were darkened to a smolder once more. But it was no longer Benjamin Wiener standing in the smoking rubble of the school. His body had transformed into something far more despicable, as if the endless reserves of evil housed in the man's soul had forced their way to the outside.

Benjamin's skin had merged with the bilious creature's and was now sickly green, nauseating, and bubbling with acidic gases. Hulking tumors of these gases simmered under his flesh, bloating his body to double its size and splitting his old trench coat in two.

Behind his red-and-blue wrestling mask were now laser eyes and sharpened chompers, courtesy of his late pet, Fido. His legs had transmogrified into anthropomorphic roller skates: wheels fashioned of smoothed phalanges and metatarsal bones, bloodied, interlaced tendons shaped into laces, and boots of diseased, toasted skin.

And, in his arms, a *guitarrón*, a gift from his master. The killer took hold of the acoustic guitar's neck and pulled outwards, unsheathing a most rock-and-roll broadsword. He held it tightly in both hands and skated out of the rubble of Barbara Falls High.

He strode into the night, lobbing Coach's head off in one clean strike on the way. The man's skeletal noggin hobbled down the street like a bowling ball with a nose, as the killer sped towards the house of cow flesh.

Chapter 19

Marvin Melville watched the analog clock above his beef pit, wishing he had the power to make time go by faster.

Instead, time seemed to have stopped altogether. His shift was over at 9:00 p.m., but he swore it had been 8:50 for the last half an hour.

This was *prom night*. He wasn't supposed to be here at Hamburger Heaven. He'd asked for this day off months ago. Yet, here he was, still at the grill, making his millionth perfectly char-grilled hamburger patty of the day instead of dancing the night away.

It was that asshole Richie Montgomery. It was common courtesy for managers to give the Hamburger Heaven high school team a day off for an event like prom, and that courtesy had extended to everyone except him.

"Marvin, buddy, you're my best fry cook," Montgomery had said, arrogant smile pasted to his face. "How would I survive without you?"

As he watched the beef patty sizzle in front of him, Marvin Melville had the sinking realization that he would be a virgin forever.

Tonight should've been the night. He had the perfect plan: ask Sandy van Thorpe to the dance floor. Nobody else was going for Sandy, so there would be no competition. She wouldn't be expecting it, and she would be swept off her feet by the romantic gesture. And then swept into the back seat of his Toyota Starlet.

Some other loser had probably beaten him to the punch by now, while he was here, stuck with a virginity as looming and indefatigable as the Soviet Union. The stress of this realization formed fourteen fresh pimples on the zit zoo he called a face.

"Earth to Melville!" The voice of Richie Montgomery hovered over him like flies on shit. "I need six more patties... and stat! Throw some fries on while you're at it! Looks like we're staying open past closing time!"

1983 Beverly Hills High Prom King Richie Montgomery loved taking out his angst on little Marvin. He'd never be able to formulate it in words, but picking on those weaker and less popular than him made him feel like he was back in the old days. Before prom queen Beverly Brittany was his wife. Before he decided not to pull out sometime in the fall of '84. Before he was gifted Richie Jr. as a result.

No, with Marvin groveling at his feet, he was the star again: the quarterback, the dreamboat, the undisputed leader of the pack.

As Marvin drew another bulk bucket of beef from the refrigerator, Richie bumped into him from behind, causing him to drop the cow meat all over the tile flooring of the kitchen.

"What the fuck do you think you're doing, Melville?" Richie yelled. "You ran right into me!"

"No... I... I'm sorry..." Marvin gasped.

"Sorry's not gonna cut it, Melville! Clean it up! And I'll make sure that beef bucket comes out of your paycheck!"

Richie walked out to the front of house, fuming at the situation he had created. He couldn't believe he was stuck here with Melville instead of boning someone from the senior class.

He stormed out of the kitchen just as a pack of customers rushed into the restaurant. He recognized a couple of them from the high school, and he started to welcome them until he saw the look on their faces. A look of pure, horrendous fear.

Jenny Hibiscus looked around the Hamburger Heaven. A few of the vinyl booths were still occupied. Three giggling sophomores sat in the back corner, one pretending to squirt ketchup on another. Near the jukebox, which played a strange, yelping rockabilly tune, was a lone drifter, hair slicked back and sporting sunglasses. A family of four sat next to the door. A young girl with blonde hair stared at Jenny, mouth wide open and hamburger in hands.

"Oh, thank god, Richie Montgomery!" Jimbo sputtered out. "If anyone would know what to do, it'd be you!"

"What in the hell happened to you guys?" Richie said. "You look like you just saw a ghost!"

"Much worse," Jane muttered behind the others.

"We need your phone, and stat." Mark Vernon took the lead on the situation.

"There's a payphone by the jukebox," Richie said.

"Damn it, man, does it look like we have quarters? The phone in the back... where is it?!" Mark yelled.

"Hey, mister, you're talking to a Hamburger Heaven branch manager! I'm going to need you to watch your tone," Richie said.

"I'll find it myself!" Jenny ran past Richie and into the kitchen.

"Wait! What in the..." Richie yelled out. Mark ran alongside Jenny, and Richie followed close behind.

Jimbo looked down at the seated family. The two kids maintained mouth-breathing eye contact with him and Jane. Ketchup dripped from the blonde girl's burger, splattering onto the table and her pink dress.

"Oh, Annie, look what you've done to your dress," her mom called out, reaching across the table with a napkin.

Behind them, the front doors smashed to bits. Glass erupted in all directions, sending a few shards into Jimbo's girthy chest and giving the seated mother a very painful, unexpected session of acupuncture. She collapsed onto her daughter's plate, squelching more ketchup onto poor Annie's dress.

Jimbo stood, horrified. He had no clue what to do. A large piece of glass had punctured his sternum, and a trickle of blood ran down his stained wife-beater. And then there was the thing in front of him.

The fear of not getting laid or having someone think he was uncool was child's play compared to the soul-fucking dread the sight of the man sent through Jimbo's bones. For this was no mere man. This was the sum of all the world's nightmares pounded together into a walking, breathing biped, dripping pure evil, and acidic snot, from every pore.

It would've haunted Jimbo's dreams for years to come if he had lived long enough to ever sleep again.

The killer walked through the remains of the

front door and unsheathed a long sword from the *guitarrón* slung across his shoulder. He ambled up to Jimbo, cherishing the look of pitiful fear on the lard-boy's face.

Jimbo could do nothing. His legs had given up on him and couldn't muster the strength to even back away from the creeping marauder. He had been overtaken by the rigor mortis of pure dread.

He watched as the man thrust his broadsword through his genital organs, up through his intestines and stomach, and between his pecs. Scorching pain erupted through his body as his heart received notice it was going to be out of a job. Gallons of blood dumped from his gooch. He averted his eyes, the sight of his gashed genitalia too much for the poor boy to handle.

"It seems you've sprung a leak," the killer said with a smile on his mangled turkey melt of a face. His voice was a pustular gurgle. "Let me tighten you up a bit."

He took the sword's headstock in both hands and twisted it forcefully, spinning the sword around Jimbo's chest like a roulette wheel, shredding his heart to bits, severing many important arteries, and leaving a massive, six-inch hole right in the middle of poor Jimbo.

Jimbo's life did not flash before his eyes, but a series of regrets did: failed attempts at touchdowns, arguments with his mother, never being passionate about anything in his worthless life, not getting any action on prom night. Soon, the shock and the pain blotted even those out.

"Lefty loosey... righty, he dies-y," the killer said. He pulled the sword back and left Jimbo to collapse to the ground.

Jane, hiding underneath a vinyl booth, watched as the deflated Jimbo fell to the floor. His dying eyes met hers one final time, before the light of consciousness inside them extinguished before her gaze. A tinge of joy tinted the fright surging through Jane's veins.

The killer swung his broadsword from side to side, flinging trails of blood onto the chessboard floor and little orphan Annie's cherubic face. A blister on his arm popped, spraying a Hadean eruption of pus onto Annie's collapsed mother, briefly waking her from her painful stupor as the skin on her back sizzled and dissolved to nothingness. She let loose one final scream as her children looked on lethargically.

The sophomores at the back of the restaurant all shrieked in unison, falling over each other to get away from the Hell engulfing them. Annie's balding dad let out a cowardly groan at the sight of his dead wife and blood-spattered daughter.

The drifter by the jukebox stood up, straightened

out his leather jacket, and reached into a chest pocket.

"*You* interrupted my meal, fucker," the man said, brandishing a switchblade from his jacket. "Now, *I'm* gonna interrupt your life."

The greaser switched open his knife and sidled up to the masked man. The killer dropped his broadsword to embrace a round of hand-to-hand combat.

The man lunged with the switchblade, but the killer was quicker, dodging the thrust and grabbing the man by the back of his leather jacket.

"They just don't make music like they used to, do they?" the killer asked. He picked the man up with ease and skated him into the jukebox across the room.

The man's head plunged through the casing of the black Seeburg. The rockabilly tune came to an abrupt halt, replaced with the calming sounds of seizing, electrocuted flesh thwapping against tile flooring. The colorful jukebox went dark as the enveloping scent of singed skin amalgamated with the aroma of juicy, medium-rare hamburgers.

And then it flashed to life once again. The sound of trumpets and *guitarrón* drowned out the teens' shrieks. The sound of *El Cazador's Mariachi de Luchador,* back from the grave.

"Now, *that's* more like it," the killer said. He

picked up his broadsword and began to two-step to the delightful mariachi sounds.

As he danced, he sliced and diced the squad of teenagers running for the exit. He split a girl's head in two like a coconut with a clean thrust of the sword. The serrated blade slid through another's face, splitting the boy's long, sharp nose and forcefully caving in his skull. He left the sword inside the boy's head in order to grab a screaming girl by the throat and blow up her head with his laser eyes. Fountains of gore splish-splashed onto the linoleum flooring.

It was mayhem. The killer swelled with joy and the lessening of societal holds. The endless string of homicides released the bonds of a decade locked in a cell, of a society who had forced him to give up his reason for living, of a world who thought of his existence as foul, antithetical to their own. Each deadly bludgeoning strengthened his resolve and brought him closer to nirvana.

Another girl tripped in the ever-expanding pool of blood and knocked herself unconscious on the chessboard floor. Benjamin turned to his face-fucking broadsword, still housed deeply into a lifeless teen skull, and brought the blade down with thunderous ferocity into the girl's spine, pinning the two friends together like a soggy shish kebab.

Jane could do nothing but clasp her mouth shut

and hide. She had been obsessed with death since her youth, but now, she was certain she'd had enough of it.

The murderer dispatched the last of the shrieking sophomores, biting through her throat with a crunch and unleashing a blood flood into his mouth. The mariachi in the background played on, the jukebox's faulty electricity occasionally dipping the tune to a 16 RPM devilish dirge. Each white tile of the chessboard floor now sported a blood-red paint job.

Dropping his victim to the ground with a thud, the killer turned his attention towards the only occupied table remaining. Dad was hyperventilating, his small son was balling in the corner of the booth, and poor Annie still had not eaten her hamburger.

"Finally… dessert," the killer said.

"I don't *care* if you're understaffed, bring everyone you've got!" Mark Vernon screamed into the telephone. "The Navy, for God's sake! The Air Force! Bomb the whole town! It's a massacre!"

Through the small, circular window in the kitchen, Richie Montgomery gawked at the grisly scene in his restaurant. His limbs twitched in epileptic spasms of mortal terror. Before this, he thought he was too young to die, too handsome, too cool. Now, the truth stared him in the face through a pan-seared wrestling mask: he was nothing but a sack of piss, shit and blood, and he was going to be killed.

"No, I'm not a 'little rascal,' and this isn't a joke! I'm a grown man, for God's sake! Now, bring tanks here, stat!" Mark continued. "Wait... what do you mean, 'I'm sexy when I talk like that'? Who is this?"

A tinny voice from the other side shouted into Mark's ear. *Your worst nightmare.*

Mark swung the phone away from his ear just in time. The receiver sparked and then exploded into pieces in his hand.

After a second, Mark looked at Jenny.

"I don't think they're coming," he murmured. "Let's escape out back. Find Jimbo's van. Move to North Dakota."

"And barricade the door! That'll buy us time!" Marvin Melville shouted from his fry cook station. He was scared to death, but knew Richie Montgomery would make his life even worse if he left the grill unmanned.

"It won't matter. The killer will follow us wherever we go. This won't end until we send him back where he came from: Hell," Jenny Hibiscus said.

The room was silent.

"Then we need weapons," Mark said.

"Melville, what have you got for us?" Jenny asked the fry cook.

"You… know my name?" Melville stammered.

"Shut your mouth and find me a meat tenderizer!" she yelled.

Marvin Melville sprung into action at the sound of a beautiful woman chastising him. He ran around the kitchen and found an array of utensils perfect for pounding, pulverizing, and punishing.

Jenny grabbed a tenderizer, Marvin armed himself with two large butcher knives, and Mark opted for a skillet in one hand and a kitchen-standard knuckle duster in the other.

"Montgomery, arm up!" Jenny yelled.

Richie Montgomery turned back towards them, tears in his eyes and uselessness wafting from him like body odor.

"But… I'm scared!" he cried.

"You hear that, everyone? Mr. Prom King is *scared.*" Jenny approached Richie. "Well then, I'm announcing a demotion here at Hamburger Heaven tonight."

She took the red-and-white manager hat off his head and threw it in a nearby trash can.

"You're the fry cook now," she said.

"Yes, ma'am!" Richie saluted his new boss and ran to his station, tail between his legs.

"And now, we wait for our special guest…" Jenny whispered.

After watching the killer split open a little girl's head and pick her brain with fork and knife, Jane had sworn off wearing all black, fantasizing about death, and living the goth lifestyle. If she survived tonight, she would spend the rest of her days listening to Wang Chung.

The family's booth was now a charcuterie board of cruelty. Guts dripped from the table, and organs decorated uneaten hamburgers. The balding father's head, carved from the inside like a Halloween pumpkin, acted as the Bacchic centerpiece.

The killer slurped up another mouthful of brain matter and slipped out of the booth, licking his fingers clean. He skated towards the kitchen door.

Jane's heart took a leap. The masked man did not know she was there. She intended to keep it that way.

"And I'll huff and I'll puff and I'll stab your house in!" the killer yelled outside the kitchen door. His gurgling voice exuded disgusting, bilious malevolence.

Inside the kitchen, Jenny, Mark, and Melvin tightened their grip on their weapons of choice. Richie Montgomery put a new batch of fries into the fry vat.

"We'll take him out," Mark whispered into Jenny's ear. "For Jeremy."

"I love it when you talk like that," Jenny said.

"I love you," Mark said.

He moved his mouth towards her mouth for a meeting of mouths. They sensually kissed each other, sending waves of love out into the air and into the gallons of beef meat spilled all over the kitchen.

Waves of love, however, were not enough to stop the murderous killer. The man aimed his optical lasers towards the kitchen doors and blew them off their hinges. One of the doors shot towards Marvin Melville, who held up his butcher knives in fear.

The force of the door thrust one of the raised blades into his greasy face, serrating through his right nostril like a honey ham and straight into his frontal lobe. He didn't even have time to wistfully rue about dying a virgin loser before he slipped into grand nothingness.

After the killer glided into the kitchen, spun a graceful pirouette, and beheaded Marvin in an explosion of grue, he looked around the room and thought of El Cazador's three pieces of advice. The three tools necessary to bring the entire world to its knees.

A monolithic creature of slime. Cow's flesh shaped into patties. A man with powers much like your own.

There were only two men left in the kitchen, and one was a crying fry cook. But the other man, the one currently tongue-kissing a teenager...

Benjamin Wiener was having a truly wonderful day, but he was disappointed he never had an encounter with the adolescent psychic who had been hijacking his mind since his escape from Shady Hills. Benjamin thought he could sway this boy towards the side of Satan.

Looking at the older man, Benjamin had a feeling deep in his bones he was of the same ilk. Which meant he held the key for unleashing the evil of El Cazador on this puny, insignificant world.

Jenny loosened herself from Mark's smooth, hearty lips. For a second, she forgot their lives were in imminent danger.

"Oh, Mark," Jenny Hibiscus muttered. She left his loving embrace and was met with the sight of Marvin Melville's brains mingling with ground beef.

"What a wonderful night," Mark said. "Absolutely horrible, but wonderful, too."

Jenny looked over at the killer, right in time to see him ready his broadsword like a javelin and toss it right towards them.

"Mark, no!" she screamed. She tossed herself to the ground and hoped Mark would do the same.

He did not. He flipped around, ready to fight, and caught a sword right in the stomach. The momentum flung him across the room, pinning him to the far wall of the kitchen.

He groaned in pain. He was stuck to the wall. Any slight movement caused excruciating pain and oozing leakage of stomach innards.

Jenny ran over to her crucified love. The sword had broken completely through his abdomen. Bits of spine peeked out of his back. The *guitarrón* was stuck an inch and a half deep into the wall behind him.

"No, Mark! This can't happen! This can't happen again!" Jenny cried.

The killer approached them. On the way, he took Richie Montgomery's face and dunked it into the vat of hot French fry grease, instantly ruining the man's perfect Prom King complexion. He held him there for thirty seconds, waiting for Richie to perfectly brown.

The fry timer dinged. The killer pulled Richie out and threw him to the ground. His face splatted into a pile of sloppy cow innards and nerd brain.

"Not for me… too many calories," the killer said.

Jenny squeezed Mark's hand. Tears ran down her youthful cheeks. Losing one love of her life tonight was hard enough, but losing two? What was this cruel joke they called reality?

"I'm going to pull the sword out!" Jenny screamed.

"No… don't…" Mark groaned, each word a momentous struggle. "Baby... just know... I'll always love you..."

"I love you too, Mark," Jenny balled. "I'll never forget the times we had together."

"Now, now, enough of that! This is *not* a love story," the killer spumed as he walked over to Jenny and Mark. "And, besides, it's my turn to talk to your lover."

"Stay away!" Jenny screamed. "You monster! You... you..."

"*Devil?*" the killer asked. He skated up to Jenny, stopping mere inches from her face. Jenny could smell the burnt, rancid flesh of his face, sense the pure evil on his breath.

"Tut, tut, don't use our Lord's name in vain," he said. "Now, if you'll excuse us for a moment..."

Benjamin pushed Jenny to the ground, slamming her head against an ice cream machine and knocking her out cold. He then wheeled over to Mark.

"Peasant, look into my eyes," the killer said, making unflinching eye contact with the fading Mark. "Deeper... deeper..."

Mark could not squirm away; the pain was too intense. He had no choice but to stare at him. At those eyes. Those eyes so black. So devoid of all goodness. All humanity.

The inescapable pull of Death's hand stopped leading Mark towards the nonexistent afterlife for precious seconds. Through his entire being, all he could sense was the darkness in those eyes.

"Now… open wide."

Mark had no control over his trembling body. His maw thrust open in compliance and his neck tilted upwards, a baby bird ready to feed.

And feed he did. The killer leaned over Mark's face and let loose a torrent of caustic vomit, luminous green and chunky with evil. The deluge canvassed his head and funneled unholy bile into his digestive system.

Mark's world disappeared in an instant. His earthly experience was far away, his fading body nowhere to be found. In a flash, he was somewhere else.

A cube-shaped room. Nearly silent except for an ambient whir, pulsating in and out like blood circling through the valves of the heart. Each of the six sides of the room shined with a different shade of neon light: yellow, red, blue, purple, green, and orange. As the whirring got louder, the intensity of the sharp colors followed suit.

The sound was more than calming, the colors more than beautiful. They were transcendent. They were the way, the *dao*. The self. Peace flowed through the cube and out of its solid walls, creating the air itself around him. Here, there was nothing to be done. No goals to be achieved or battles to be won.

There was just him. There was just everything.

"Welcome to your mind," a voice from above announced. Mark recognized it from somewhere, but he couldn't place it. Come to think of it... who was *he*?

He didn't need to look around him or try to feel the calming sensations. No, he wasn't *in* this strange, glowing room... he *was* the room. His consciousness had expanded beyond a simple body and was now everything he saw around him.

"Exactly right," the voice said. "This room is you. You are this room. But this room is also me."

The red side of the cube began to shine with newfound intensity.

What is happening?

"This is your brain on *Satan*."

The entire cube quaked violently. Mark felt his entire self being thrown around, as if he were a bug trapped in a mason jar cruelly shaken by a small child.

"Feel Him guide you. Feel Him *enter* you."

A crack appeared in the pink side of the cube. The split widened, sending chunks of the cube spinning and whirling around the room. The neon lights flickered on and off, and the whirring swelled to a fever pitch, no longer content or rhythmic. The calm, alien atmosphere took on a shaded unease.

"*El Satanás* is going deeper... deeper..."

The sound of machines grew intolerable. Each side of the mind cube gave in to the force behind it, crumbling like cheap plaster. Mark could feel his soul falling apart in similar fashion.

The feeling was so much worse than the regret of waking up next to a cheap piece of flesh, or the withdrawals of a night without his fix. His soul itself was eroding, his eternal being quaking in terror.

"Hey, Benjamin!"

Thrust from Mark's mind, Benjamin Wiener snapped back to reality, just in time to watch Crazy Jane lift a butcher knife high and thrust it as hard as she could into his crotch.

The masked psychopath let loose a wail of pain. Instead of blood, the wound leaked acidic sludge onto Mark's right leg, boiling and cooking it like veal.

"You *bitch*," the killer groaned.

"You're no devil," Jane said, backing away from the bent-over, hulking horror. "You're just trash, like all the rest of us."

Blood ran from the man's mouth as he smiled. "I was *right* in the middle of something. Something more important than all of us combined."

"Well, your meeting just got canceled," a voice said from behind him.

Benjamin spun again once more to meet a large, wooden cutting board swinging right towards his face.

The killer fell backwards, the impact cracking open his jaw. The momentum of jawbone against teeth splintered his front incisors and sent them rocketing down his throat.

Benjamin Wiener's face was not in good shape. Sizzling blisters crossed every inch of his homely mug. His mouth was covered in blood, acidic slime and remnants of shattered teeth.

Jenny Hibiscus was determined to make it look much, much worse. She tightened her grip on the paddle-style cutting board and ran towards him. She dropped to her knees, raised the board to the sky, and delivered blow after crushing blow to his face.

His skull was demolished easily. Each smack further caved in his forehead and sent bits of neon, gooey brain matter splashing across the floor. One eye was squashed like a grape, the other crisped shut completely like a rabid case of pinkeye. Ocular fluid drained down into his mouth and mixed with crumbs of splintered teeth to form a delicious cocktail. Jenny smashed the paddle into his face until there were no recognizable features left, only a pile of organic head mush.

Jenny only stopped smashing when the paddle

snapped in two. The larger end lodged itself in the pile of Benjamin like an American flag declaring stolen land. She threw the other half across the room and collapsed onto the floor, her tears of rage and despair showering the ground.

Jane walked towards her, knelt to the ground, and wrapped her in a hug.

They had done it. They had killed the murderous killer.

Chapter 20

The room no longer resembled a cube. Its edges were crumpled into origami, and the fluorescent colors had faded to a simple matte red.

Mark Vernon wanted only to scream. His mind could not form coherent enough thoughts to comprehend what was happening around him. His soul, tattered, defiled, held on to the last remaining ribbons of sanity, facing a plunge into a fate much worse than the void of death.

Torturous visions baked wounds of agony unimaginable to creatures as vacuous as humans. Even in times of suicidal despondency and blackened rage, one still has a last resort, an exit plan from their weak, tormented body. In the abstracted cube, there was no escape. It was Hell, stretched out past the vastness of cosmos and slingshot back into every proton of existence.

There was no breath to gasp, no vision to obscure, no sense capable of distracting Mark Vernon's soul from its dissolution into accursed bile.

And no way to stop that bile from seeping from its cage, no way to calm its desire to expurgate our world of all we call good.

Wrapped in Jenny Hibiscus' arms, Jane looked at the chaos around her. The killer's brains and chunks were splattered across all four walls of the Hamburger Heaven kitchen. Her Doc Martens had been stained by pink goo after stepping in Marvin Melville. A past prom king lay tempura-d on the ground in a pile of gore and viscera.

It was hellish, more disturbing and vile than anything her dark mind could have imagined. But now, it was over.

Jenny breathed deeply and regained her composure. She got up from the ground using the split-open skull in front of her for balance.

"We did it," Jenny answered, breathing heavily. Bashing in heads was a great cardio workout.

"I wonder if there's… anyone left in this whole *town*," Jane said.

"Our graduation ceremony sure will be quick," Jenny answered.

"I'm not going to stick around to find out."

They swept back into each other's arms, a beacon of love in a still life of horror.

Her head resting on Jenny's left shoulder, Jane stared at Mark Vernon's pinned body. Their savior was no more, slumped over in the stillness of expiration. She felt a tinge of compassion towards the man, who had come here only to help and paid the ultimate cost.

But, then, he breathed.

Mark Vernon's vomit-covered face sucked in air with desperation, as if trying to suck up the entire room's oxygen. It was a belabored, pained breath, the inhalation of one not used to the exercise.

His head slowly raised itself to the world. And Jane stared into the face of someone who was not Mark Vernon.

She backed away from Jenny.

Mark's eyes were deep black and devoid of anything resembling humanity. From his wide-open lips dripped bile-lined drool, and from inside his mouth shined a hellish red light. His puppet maw stretched wider and wider until his jawbone cracked open. Still, it continued to grow, and the red light from within grew brighter, brighter, closer, closer...

There was only one shade of red as deep and crimson as the light coming from inside Mark Vernon: the red of eternal hellscape.

"No... no... no..." Jane repeated.

Jenny spun around and nearly fainted at the sight. Mark's arms reached for his jawbone and finished the job, tearing the lower half of his face right off.

His skin ripped apart like putty, the hellish circle inside of him burning a brighter shade of fiery red each passing second.

"What the hell is..." Jenny started to ask before Mark's entire body, starting with what remained of his face, was swallowed whole by the vortex forming in his mouth.

One second, she was face-to-face with one of her two true loves. The next, all that remained was a yawning void, a portal to a dimension she wanted nothing to do with.

A pillar of flame shot outwards from the vortex. The sound of pained screaming and power tools filled the room, echoing out of the fiery pit. Liquefied drippings of skin and muscle leaked onto the tile flooring below.

"Come on, Jenny! We have to go!" Jane yelled, starting to run towards the front of house.

Jenny turned to leave with her. But something scratchy was holding on to her ankle.

It was the killer's hand, wrapped tightly around her.

Impossible, she thought. The man's head was only a pile of slop, but he still had a deathly grip on her ankle, as if his hands were made out of glue. She pulled and pulled towards the door, but she couldn't move. The man was dead weight, and lots of it.

Then, it started to rise.

The killer's bloated, mutated body floated, as if propelled by helium, up into the air. While the mashed remains of his face stayed strewn across the ground like the remains of a highway motorcyclist, the rest of him was levitating towards the ceiling.

Jenny yelled out to Jane for help. The floating corpse had a vice grip on her ankle and she lost her stepping, falling back into a pile of meat. As the body rose, she found herself being carried to the ceiling feet first. She grabbed one of the legs of the fry station and held out the other hand towards Jane.

At this point, Jane accepted what she saw without hesitation. The killer was now a headless, floating corpse and a pit of Hell just opened up in the corner of Hamburger Heaven? *Sounds like a Friday in Barbara Falls.*

She ran over and clamped on to her new friend's hand, tugging with all her limited strength. Still, the killer's headless body floated higher. It now hovered almost parallel with the ceiling, a rotting balloon running out of space to float.

Pull as she might, Jane could not break the dead man's grip on Jenny's ankle. And the groans coming from the ungodly, glowing portal were starting to worry her.

The temperature in the room was also rising, and

fast. Sweat dripped from Jane's temple, and the condensation forming on her hands made holding onto Jenny even harder. The beef, brain, and blood around her all started to sizzle and cook, producing a feast of pure horror.

That's when the first hand came out of the portal.

One by one, a series of horrifying ghouls, their faces amalgamations of hundreds of dead men and women still screaming in endless pain, scratched their way through the Hell hole into the restaurant. Their claws, razor-sharp fingernails sprouting from diseased, blue-green skin, dug into the tile flooring, each puncture producing horrible scraping sounds.

And each movement brought them closer and closer to Jane.

"Oh, Jesus! Jenny! There's more coming!" Jane yelled. Jenny screamed. Granpappy Hibiscus had not trained her for this.

Jane refused to let go. Without Jenny, she didn't know if she would have had made it through this night so far. She intended to return the favor.

The pit demons groaned in hunger. Every inch of their putrid patches of flesh were scabbed in multitudes of cavities, each one the mouth of a dead sinner. Each set of lips screamed in agony with every step towards the helpless girls.

As the demons approached, Jane kicked out at

one of them. The being lost its stiff, rigor mortis balance, knocked into another horrid zombie and sent them both rocketing noiselessly back into the vortex. Flame exploded out of the hole as if to ease digestion.

But three more ghastly beings crawled out to take their place. The pitiful noises echoing from the cavernous hellscape suggested there were many, many more behind them.

"Whatever happens, Jenny... you're my best friend!" Jane said.

"You're my best friend, too!" Jenny cried, hours of trauma having erased Sarah Farrow from her mind.

The touching moment was interrupted by a sharp, subterranean cackling. Jenny looked towards the new undead arrival to Hamburger Heaven, freshly unearthed from its hellish grave, as its stomach burst open in a splash of gore. The moaning zombie's abdominal wound stretched and pulled, until two miniature hands crawled their way out of the hellspawn's gut.

Next was its head. A tiny, orange horned being, with sharpened, shark-like rows of teeth and neon red peepers. It jumped the rest of the way out of the being. It was a miniature devil, all of six inches tall.

Jenny could hardly believe her eyes as the sentient action figure slithered on all fours up the ceiling, across the suspended corpse of Benjamin Wiener, and onto her clasped leg. It poked her bare skin with its claws and cackled another demonic laugh.

"Oh... que hermosa," the thing squeaked.

"Fucking Jesus Christ!" Jenny shouted. Her bloodcurdling scream tore open her vocal chords.

Jane lost her grip on Jenny's arms, leaving the girl swining back and forth from the killer's floating pillar of a body. She turned to run towards the front door but was tripped by a ghoul grasping at her leg. She collapsed to the ground, pounds of hamburger meat and Marvin Melville cushioning her fall.

The devilish imp crawled over Jenny's chest and onto her face, licking the side of her chin with its pointed tongue. She recoiled in disgust and tried to smack the imp away with her hands to no avail. Her attempts only made the demon cackle louder.

"Me encanta cuando peleas, mi amor," the demon laughed.

Jane tried to claw away from the approaching ghouls, but all she had to grab on to was ground beef. She scratched at the tile floor underneath, snapping two of her fingernails. One of the ghouls began to overtake her and crawl over her thin body. The smell of death raped her nose cavity.

The little devil on Jenny's face took one of its claws and dug it deep into her cheek, latching on like a meat hook. She screamed loudly. It ripped free its claw to grip on to Jenny's upper lip, then scurried over to grasp on to the other lip with its second hand.

Jenny clenched her teeth, screaming with her mouth closed, as the imp stuck its claws between her two sets of chompers.

For its size, the devil was extraordinarily strong. It pried open her mouth, letting loose Jenny's silent screams. As she was opened wider and wider, the devil climbed in, muffling Jenny's cries. Its evil claws poked deep into her tongue and the roof of her mouth.

She felt her throat being lacerated from the inside, like she was swallowing animate glass. She tried to make herself puke up the tiny demon, but all that would regurgitate was the blood and gore choking her windpipe.

The naked, leathery blue skin of the undead demon chafed against Jane and pinned her to the floor. The screaming of past sinners wafted from the being's diseased body. The mouths littered across its rotten flesh licked and kissed her legs and chest as the awful, necrotic head got closer and closer to her screaming, twisting face.

When it fully mounted her, the demon grabbed

Jane's face and twisted it towards its worm-rotted mouth. She couldn't move. She knew the hellspawn could snap her neck like a stick in one swift gesture.

The ghoul opened its mouth, crumbling its jaw to dust. Maggots poured from the opening, and the creature's rotted tongue, a slab of slimy, green cheese, fell onto Jane's chest with a splat.

Jane stared into the ghoul's dead, blackened eyes. In a kaleidoscopic surge, she witnessed all seven circles of Hell at once. Flesh ripped from screaming bodies with pitchforks, meat hooks and automated machines. Tunnels of fire-singed pubic hair and branded genitals. Men dipped into boiling vats of acid, then left to desiccate on steaming granite.

As soon as it began, the subliminal flash was gone. As was her sanity. The vision had snuffed out any belief in good still left in her, obliterated her desire to live one single second longer in an existence this cruel.

She felt the pain of victims of violent lust throughout history. She held the feeling of those on the brink, those whose urge to blow their brains to bits finally outweighed the fear of what came after. She saw her mother, destroyed by her attempts at loving a daughter so distant and ghastly.

Crazy Jane let loose a single sob. Her lips split open in an expression of morose dismay.

As she did so, black sludge poured from the demon's mouth and down her throat, choking her as she struggled to swallow and digest the hellish muck. As the sludge caked her face, Jane lost all ability to see, smell, or hear. Her only sensations were infinite blackness and cavernous sorrow. Soon, even that fell away.

The pain became too much for Jenny Hibiscus. Inside her, the imp scratched out her vocal cords and settled in near her heart. Her arms fell limp over her head, the will to live fading alongside her vision. The short life she lived flit across her eyes like a mountain breeze and faded as quickly as it came.

Spirits of ghastly, demonic souls floated through the vacuous portal, briefly turning the restaurant into a congregation of evil spirits, a Hamburger *Hell.*

From there, they floated off into the night, flying to destinations far and wide, eager to wreak torment on earthly souls.

The naked ghouls crawled back from whence they came, plummeting into Hell's pit. Benjamin Wiener's headless body combusted into ash, the remains sprinkling the mounds of cooked cow and teen meat below like oregano. The fiery portal had lit a blaze in the kitchen that now traveled to all corners of the restaurant, setting the beloved staple of the town ablaze.

It would soon conflagrate completely, crumbling into mere memories of delicious, charbroiled quarter-pounders.

As the final ghoul fell back into Hell, the pit spat out one last geyser of fire before sealing itself up, disappearing into its own inertia. The infernal screams of damned souls and the stench of seared flesh fell away until Hamburger Heaven took on a complete silence. The sounds of collapsing plaster and fire alarms were swallowed up by the horrors of that night, replaced with a vacuum of noiselessness.

Jane and Jenny lay motionless on the ground. From Jenny Hibiscus' chest rose and fell a series of weak breaths. They made no sound, though, because Hamburger Heaven was silent.

And so it stayed.

Chapter 21

Hours later, the county fire department made its way to fight the flames engulfing Hamburger Heaven and Barbara Falls High. They fought against the conflagration all night, stamping out the last embers as the sun rose over the town.

It was another pleasant April morning in the forested town, but none of its residents took advantage of the nice weather. Instead, they mourned and wondered what monstrous events had taken place at the B.F. High prom the night before.

The state police force tried to make sense of the disaster, but came up empty. The parts of the school which remained untouched by fire brought only more questions. Mangled, naked bodies hung in the auditorium. One entire hallway was flooded with mysterious black slime.

The police knew but one thing: fires don't strip people naked and perform genital mutilation on young girls.

Parents were herded to the town's police station,

where they awaited information on the well-being of their sons and daughters. No one left with a smile on their face. Attempting to soften the blow, other town members baked many, many cakes for the now-childless parents. However, losing the only light in your sad, sad lives leaves a pit in one's stomach that substantially decreases any enjoyment of cake.

The bodies at Hamburger Heaven were more easily identified. Among the remains, they found senior Jane Canens, star linebacker Jimbo McKinney, not-star accountant Tom Davis, his wife and two children, and a drifter nicknamed "Slippo Jones" for his ability to escape from the law. The police made sure to arrest his corpse for their own dignity.

Mr. & Mrs. Hibiscus waited for information on their daughter, but none came. They assumed, as many parents did, their little girl was lost amongst the rubble, another pile of bones in the unholy catacombs once known as Barbara Falls High.

In Salt Lake City, Kriegshorn Oil & Gas mourned the disappearance of their senior advisor, Mark Vernon, never realizing he had traveled to Barbara Falls. One day, he had a headache, went home, and never returned. His wife of seven years received a significant life insurance compensation, and Mark was replaced by an overseas hire they could pay half the salary.

As bodies were identified, Barbara Falls made a valiant effort to get through the tragedy together as a community. That effort was soon replaced by rampant alcoholism and repression of feelings. While these healthy responses were to be expected, something more horrible simmered under the surface.

Barbara Fallians felt a change in their community after the tragedy. Drivers no longer waved at passersby on Main Street; in fact, one incident of Main St. road rage resulted in a young woman bludgeoned to death with a tire iron. Armed robbery rates skyrocketed. The local pastor left town after multiple threats on his life.

There was seemingly no explanation for the wave of chaos. Unresolved trauma? Or a deeper evil coursing through the town's veins?

The few residents who read newspapers knew these deviations were not limited to Barbara Falls. Across the United States, across the mysterious countries elsewhere in the world, rape, murder, and torture were becoming more commonplace than copies of Linda Ronstadt albums in record store bargain bins.

Closer to home, though, the town's valiant namesake still babbled, undaunted. The waterfall became a popular stop for mourning parents and concerned townspeople yearning to get away, trying to forget, looking to the glory of nature for a reprieve from their daily hell.

Trouble is, many of them never returned.

Some said they fled the town, aiming for greener pastures elsewhere. But others told tales of a beautiful, ghostly, blonde teen who wandered the woods around Barbara Falls. She could be seen on the side of the road, waving frantically for a ride, or by the water, searching for something gone missing.

If anyone was friendly enough to help her, it would be their final act of kindness.

Whether they believed the tales or not, most of the town once again started to avoid the falls. Those who needed to make the drive through the forest did so racked with anxiety and fear, their radios cranked up loud to drown out the whispers they heard from the woods.

The eerie, ghostly whispers of mariachi.

www.ingramcontent.com/pod-product-compliance
Lightning Source LLC
Chambersburg PA
CBHW051310130726
47987CB00004B/1742

* 9 7 9 8 9 8 9 0 4 0 8 0 3 *